THE ESCAPE CLAUSE

THE KELLER FAMILY SERIES ~ BOOK TEN

BERNADETTE MARIE

5 PRINCE PUBLISHING

ISBN DIGITAL: 978-1-63112-100-5

ISBN PRINT: 978-1-63112-101-2

The Escape Clause, Bernadette Marie

Copyright Bernadette Marie 2014-2022

Published by 5 Prince Publishing

4th version/printing 2022

12-8

For Stan,
Thank goodness you were my Escape Clause!

ACKNOWLEDGMENTS

For Stan who was my escape nearly 25 years ago. Thank goodness you were under that window!

For my 5 Princes, you are my greatest inspiration when it comes to building the dynamics of these families.

For Mom, Dad, and Anni thank you for all things.

For Connie, Clare, and Marie who had bets against me? Hands high~because you're all here holding my hand it all got done.

For June and Connie who dot every I and cross every T, thank you.

ALSO BY BERNADETTE MARIE

Date for Hire

THE DEVEREAUX FAMILY SERIES

Kennedy Devereaux

Chase Devereaux

Max Devereaux

Paige Devereaux

FUNERALS AND WEDDINGS SERIES

Something Lost

Something Discovered

Something Found

Something Forbidden

Something New

THE ESCAPE CLAUSE

CHAPTER 1

$\mathcal{H}$ospitals were Avery's least favorite place to be. She had to admire her father for choosing a career that had him bound to them for so many years.

As the day of her birthday slipped away and a new day began, she sat in the waiting room with her family.

She wondered if this was the similar scene twenty-six years ago when she and her cousin Spencer were born. Surely her parents were surrounded by family, and in another room her aunt and uncle were surrounded by the same family.

Spencer was only an hour older than Avery was, and they'd shared every birthday together since that first one. And now, after their celebration, her cousin Christian's wife Victoria was in one room of the hospital in labor, and her cousin Ed and his wife Darcy were in another.

She'd watched as Ed and Christian's parents, her aunt Madeline and uncle Carlos, went from room to room. Ed and Christian's sister Clara sat across from Avery rubbing her very pregnant stomach.

The Keller family was being bombarded with babies, and now her cousin Tyler and his wife Courtney were expecting too.

For a very brief moment, she felt a pang of jealousy rip through her. Would she ever know this moment? Would she ever have that man who would bring her to this moment?

Pete walked up next to her and held out a paper cup of coffee from the vending machine. "Best we can get at one in the morning."

She graciously took it as he sat down. "Thanks. My head is still swimming from all the wine I drank."

He gave her a small nudge. "Lush," he said with a chuckle and then began to blow on his coffee.

For a moment, Avery just watched him. Pete Grant had been her dearest friend her entire life. He'd bowed down and played dress up a few times. He'd taught her how to bounce a soccer ball on her forehead. Thinking back, he'd even canceled his own prom date to take her when her date backed out. He was that kind of friend.

And now here he was, sitting in a hospital at one o'clock in the morning waiting out babies with her and her family.

She rested her head on his shoulder and he pressed his head to hers.

It was nice to be so comfortable around a friend. He was easing that jealousy she'd been feeling. Someday he'd make someone a good husband.

AROUND TWO O'CLOCK, Christian walked out into the waiting area rubbing his eyes. Their aunt Arianna jumped to her feet.

"Well?"

He shook his head. "Her contractions stopped. They're going to let her rest for a little bit and see how it goes. If they need to induce her, they will do that later today. The baby is ready, just not cooperating."

Avery was sure everyone in the room, who was awake, wanted to make some comment to the lack of cooperation and aim it at Christian. However, the look on his face—that look of worry—had them all remaining quiet.

Victoria had lost their first child. As Avery's father had told them, it just happened. But Avery was sure neither of them ever got over it—how could they?

She turned her face into Pete's shoulder so that his shirt caught the few tears that were threatening to spill.

"Are you okay?" His voice was a whisper and so gentle.

"I'm just worried for them."

Pete moved his hand over hers and gave it a squeeze. "Everything is going to be okay. Babies have their own agenda, and it isn't ours."

She supposed he knew what he was talking about. He had four sisters and a brother. His family was as close as her extended family. She, of course, was an only child. It had never felt like that though. There probably wasn't a day in her life where she hadn't seen one of her cousins, aunts, or uncles.

As she turned her hand over in his and locked their fingers, she realized they were both blessed to have that. Now all they had to do was find that right person, for each of them, that could make them happy forever.

A few minutes later, Ed staggered into the waiting room. The clothes he'd worn to Avery's party were now under a paper robe. He had a mask down under his chin and a paper hat over his hair. Darcy had gone into labor at the same time as Victoria. However, their baby was breech and more excited to meet everyone as she was scheduled the following week to have a Caesarean. But, now was a good time too, Avery thought as she looked at her cousin with his enormous grin.

Christian was the first to step to him. "Well?"

"She's here. She's here!"

Christian pulled his brother to him in a hug that had Avery's eyes filling fuller with tears.

"I'm happy for you," Christian said patting his brother's back and looking at him. "She's healthy and Darcy is okay?"

"She's perfect. Oh, she's perfect. And Darcy is wonderful. She's in recovery and Mom and Regan are with her." He looked around the room.

In the corner, Ed found his father asleep in a chair with his daughter Emily asleep on his shoulder.

Avery watched as Ed moved to them. He touched his father's hand, waking him up.

"She's here. A little girl, Dad."

Avery's uncle Carlos smiled a wide smile, careful not to move.

"I know she'll never understand this, but I want to take her to see her sister." He rolled the little girl from his father's shoulder and she stirred. "Hey, big sister. Let's go see your baby sister."

Avery wasn't sure that at ten months little Emily, whom Ed and Darcy had adopted, had a clue as to what was going on, but they'd all remember.

Pete turned to look at Avery.

"You look exhausted. Why don't I take you home for a while? It doesn't sound like Victoria is going to have her baby tonight."

She hated the thought of leaving, but she knew it made sense. She could go home, get a few hours sleep, and be right back there in the morning to wait out another baby.

Avery looked at Clara uncomfortably seated in the chair across from her and Warner rubbing her back to comfort her.

That jealous pang hit her chest again.

"Okay, let me say goodbye to my parents."

CHAPTER 2

*P*ete watched as Avery hugged everyone that would stay and wait. He'd have to call his own mother in the morning. Avery's family had been close to his family for years. They'd want to know about Ed's little girl, whom he'd forgotten to get her name. Maybe they didn't have one yet.

Avery yawned as she walked toward him. He placed his arm around her waist as they walked to the elevator.

When the doors opened, they stepped in, and he hit the button for the lobby.

"Exciting night," Pete said.

Avery nodded. "Did you see the new jewelry on Julie's finger?" She made the comment perhaps a bit too snippy. "No wonder Spencer left our birthday party early."

"I thought it was the pink and black cake you made him have —again."

That brought a bit of a smile to her lips. She did like to torment her birthday-twin cousin by designing the color theme every year—pink and black.

Pete took her hand and brought it to his lips. Pressing a kiss

5

to her fingers, he said, "I can't think of a better reason to leave a party than to get engaged. If that's what they did."

"Why else would she have a ring like that?"

He shrugged. But he knew that Spencer was all class. Right now, it was Darcy and Ed's moment, and soon it would be Christian and Victoria's moment. He'd have time to share the news if there was any.

When the doors opened, Pete kept hold of Avery's hand and walked her to his car in the parking garage. She was silent on the walk. He opened the door for her and waited until she was comfortable before walking around and getting in himself.

"Thank you for being here with me," she said wiping tears from her eyes. "I seem to be a little emotional about it all."

"You deserve to be. But, Avery, you know there isn't anywhere I'd rather be than with you."

That caused her to chuckle. "You need a woman," she retorted as he started the engine and backed out of the parking space.

"I guess if one comes along. For now, I'll just spend my time with you."

She smiled at him. "I'm lucky to have you."

"Likewise."

She reached for his hand and held it in hers. "I don't want to be alone tonight. Will you stay with me?"

Pete shrugged. "I could. Do you have a fan for that spare room? It gets really hot in there."

Avery nodded. "Yes." She then leaned over and rested her head on his shoulder. "You're too good to me."

"I know that."

"I'm going to miss you when I move away," she said and he felt every muscle in his body tense.

"I was hoping by now you'd changed your mind."

The thought of her moving to France to run some vineyard that her grandfather, whom she didn't know very well, had bought for her had his blood hot. Her parents weren't going to like it either. Hell, he didn't like it too much. But what could he say?

Pete had longed for her as long as he could remember and she didn't seem to have the same feelings. What more could he do than to support his dearest friend in her new adventure?

Perhaps while she was gone, his focus would change and he would find that woman she was always saying he deserved.

"I was thinking, when you go, maybe I could rent the house from your aunt. My lease is up next month and I'd like something a little bigger."

She looked up at him and smiled. "I think that would be nice. I'm sure Julie will be moving out soon." She chuckled again. "Maybe the woman of your dreams will move in. It worked for Ed and for Spencer."

"Maybe," he said turning down her street.

He drove down the alley to the back of Avery's house and parked next to her car.

"Maybe I should just head home," he said. "It's really late and you need some sleep."

She shook her head. "I don't want to be alone."

He knew that, but he just needed some space. The move to France weighed too heavily on him, and the fact that she didn't even see him as anything other than a friend was wearing on him too.

The motion lights on the back porch turned on as Avery opened the car door. "Please come in," she said softly. "If you don't stay that's fine. Just keep me company."

It was already three o'clock in the morning. She'd want to head back to the hospital early. He might as well stay.

Pete opened his door and stepped out as she shut her door and dug through her purse for her keys.

As he walked around the car, she looked up at him. The light behind her gave her a glow, and at that moment, he thought she might be more beautiful than any other time in her life.

"You looked amazing tonight, by the way," he said, not resisting when the urge to touch her hair took over.

"Thank you. I had a fun night." She pressed her lips together. "I was thinking we could go back to the hospital around nine."

Pete nodded. "Sure," he agreed when she included him in her plans.

"And I was hoping maybe you'd hold me all night," she said quickly as if she'd been holding in those words all night.

There was a flash in her eyes and he wasn't sure she knew it had happened. But he'd caught it.

Pete moved in closer to her, resting his hands on her hips. "You want me to sleep in your bed with you?" His voice cracked as he said the words he never thought he'd say.

She nodded. "Just to hold me. I feel—I don't know what I feel."

He did. He knew exactly what it was. She was feeling alone even though all the people who loved her surrounded her. They were all moving in different directions with their lives now. Of course, most of them were moving toward families of their own. It was obvious, as she'd pointed out, that even Spencer and Julie were moving in that direction. That put Avery in a very unfamiliar place—alone.

He'd felt that way when his younger sister got married too. Pete was officially the last single Grant. But it wasn't so bad. He had a slew of nieces and nephews and plenty of couches to crash on. But they were both—alone.

Pete followed her up to the house and as she pushed open the door, he closed and locked it behind him.

"Do you want something to drink?" she asked.

"I'm really tired. I think I'd rather just turn in."

Avery nodded, but she didn't walk further into the house. Instead, she looked up at him. Her eyes were tired, her mascara wiped away, and her nose was red from the tears she'd shed during the night.

Completely exhausted, she still radiated.

"C'mon, old lady," he joked at her new age. "Let's get you to bed."

He took her hand and began to pull her through the kitchen, but she tugged against him.

Pete stopped and looked at her, but the way she looked up at him he knew there were no words. For a long moment, he stood there gazing upon her.

"Avery…"

She stepped to him. "What are we doing?"

"Going to bed," he said simply.

She shook her head. "There's more isn't there?"

God, hadn't he always hoped there was?

Pete moved to her so they were nearly pressed together. "Avery, what are you saying?"

"I don't want to be alone."

"I know. That's why I'm here."

Avery stepped to him and rested her hands on his chest. "You're always here."

Pete nodded. Here was where he always wanted to be.

She slid her hands up and around his neck. Instinctively, he wrapped his arms around her.

"Pete, we've never kissed."

"Sure we…"

"Not like a real kiss."

Pete licked his lips because his mouth had suddenly gone dry. "Friends don't kiss like that."

"Some do. Tiffany and Spencer did."

She mentioned her cousin and his friend with benefits. That was until he fell in love with Julie.

"You and I are different. We don't want that to come between us," he reminded her.

Avery's fingers were playing in his hair and suddenly the three o'clock hour must be messing with them. They seriously weren't caressing each other in the kitchen and talking about kissing were they?

Not that there was any space between them, but she closed it and now their bodies were pressing together.

"Everyone has been reminding me lately that you and I have been inseparable since we were little." Her fingers were now caressing his ear.

"That's what the title of 'best friends' means," he said, swallowing hard because he'd always wanted to be more.

"Pete," her voice trailed off as she gazed up at him. "Kiss me one time as if we were a couple—as if you loved me."

He hesitated because he wasn't sure he could do this just once. If he kissed her now, he wouldn't want to stop with just one kiss. He couldn't give her what she wanted.

"Avery…"

"Shhh," she pressed her finger to his lips. "Just kiss me."

He'd never denied Avery anything in all the years they'd known each other. Certainly, he wasn't going to start disappointing her now.

Pete lifted his hand to her cheek and drew her in.

The moment their lips touched that spark he knew burned inside of him exploded in a brilliant white light behind his eyelids. The feel of her, the taste of her, was more wonderful than he'd ever dreamed—and he had dreamed of it.

Her tongue slipped through his lips and danced with his as her arms tightened around him and his around her.

The moan that escaped her throat had him yearning to continue this simple request forever.

CHAPTER 3

A series of explosions were going off in Avery's body. She seriously hadn't expected that when she'd asked Pete to kiss her. She was lonely and overwhelmed—and now she was floating on some sensory cloud that had her pulling him closer.

Pete maneuvered them a few steps so that Avery was backed against the refrigerator. His fingers pressed into her hips as if he were afraid to move them any further.

Avery wound her fingers into his dark hair as she devoured the taste, the smell, the feel of him pressed against her.

She worked her tongue against his and the fireworks going off in her head made every nerve in her body pulse in explosions. They were pressed so close, she could feel the pounding of his heart against her breasts and it only made her body more pliant to push against his.

It wasn't what she'd expected when she'd asked him to kiss her. Where had this all come from? This was a maddening erotic kiss that had her knees weak, and her heart beating an erratic rhythm in her chest.

She'd suck in a breath if she could, but it was as if his mouth on hers was the only thing keeping her alive at the moment. Fear of pulling away kept her right where she was—pressed beneath him.

Pete's fingers loosened and she was afraid he was going to break this amazing kiss. Would he regret it and want to leave? Did it mean anything to him because it was meaning a hell of a lot to her—she hadn't thought it possible.

Instead of pulling away, he moved his hands slowly up the sides of her torso, over her ribs, and rested them just as his thumbs reached the spot just under her breasts.

With his mouth still working against hers, she managed a breath of anticipation waiting for him to touch her. That glorious moment when his hands would explore her.

The need was almost so great she could feel her moving to optimize the opportunity.

The kiss continued, but his hands remained.

That wouldn't do. Avery needed more. She needed to be with him. A desire to touch him fueled the fire in her core. The longing for him to touch her had her gasping for that necessary breath that was eluding her.

When they both had run out of air, Pete collapsed against her pressing her back against the metal of the refrigerator door. His face rested in the crevice of her neck.

Their chests heaved to catch up with the air that whooshed into their lungs. Her fingers were still caught in his hair and his hands rested on her rib cage, just holding her. But when his thumbs began to make soft circles against the fabric of her dress, she thought she was going to explode.

"Pete," his name burst out on a breath. "I want more."

His lips moved to her neck and he feathered her skin with soft kisses right at her pulse point.

Was it possible for a woman to melt into a puddle under a man's touch? Avery was sure that was what was going to happen.

Pete then rested his forehead against hers. His lips were only a glorious beat from her, but he didn't kiss her.

"Avery. Sweet Avery."

His eyes were closed still and his body still pushed up against hers. He wasn't going to walk away from this was he? She couldn't. She needed him right now more than she'd ever needed anything—anyone.

"Pete, please," the words carried the hunger she was feeling. "More."

His eyes opened and they had grown dark with desire, which only made her want him more.

"It's more than this. You know that," he said on a raspy breath. "I want it too. I always have."

"Carry me upstairs." She nipped his lips with a kiss that made him moan.

"Not just tonight. It can't be just tonight."

Was he making sense?

"Okay," she let the words out on a sigh as his hands moved to her back and slid down over her bottom.

Pete moved his lips back to her neck and she arched up to him. God, she'd never wanted anything more than to be under this man she cherished.

He lifted her to his hips and she wrapped her legs tightly around him as their mouths came together again. Now the kisses were flashes of hunger. This was greater than need now. It was survival, this she was sure, because it felt as if her heart would explode if she didn't feed on him.

Easily and swiftly, he carried her up the stairs with his mouth still working against hers. When he reached her bedroom, he lowered her to the bed without breaking their kiss.

The feel of him atop of her lifted that weight of loneliness from her chest. Something else filled it now, but she'd think about that later. Right now she wanted to get him undressed. Everything was about to change.

CHAPTER 4

*P*ete fought every animal urge to not just lift the skirt of Avery's dress and take her in one quick, fulfilling moment.

She needed more. She deserved more.

Her fingers were on the buttons of his shirt making quick work to open it and push the fabric from his skin.

They'd been swimming hundreds of times since they were little. She'd seen him, been in his arms as he threw her into the water. But her hands pressed against his bare flesh now made him light headed.

He could die now and he'd be happy.

Avery's skirt had bunched up between them. Those perfectly yoga toned thighs were exposed beneath him. The flash of her pink panties caught his attention and he was surprised he didn't black out.

This was Avery beneath him, not just some woman he thought he cared for. This was the woman he loved more than any other—his truest friend.

Pete looked down at her. Those lust filled eyes were dark and her lips parted in a swollen pink pout.

Pete gripped her hands in his and moved his mouth to hers again. She wiggled beneath him and he had to tell her. He'd regret it forever if he didn't let her know how he felt.

"Avery," her name was a whisper on his lips as she rubbed her body against him. "I have to tell you." He pressed a kiss to her ear lobe.

"Pete, don't stop. Please," she pleaded. "I want this. I really do."

Oh, he knew that. There wasn't a part of him that didn't feel that.

He eased up so he could look down at her, their fingers still locked together. It was now or never.

"I love you. I've always loved you."

Her eyes flashed. Regret? Acceptance? He wasn't sure as she stared up at him, her chest heaving beneath him.

"Pete…"

"Not just for tonight, remember." What was that twinge in his chest? Heartbreak? He braced himself for it.

The glaze in her eyes softened and those lips curved into a smile. "I love you too."

The words from her lips nearly shot tears into his eyes. No, it wasn't the time for it. He took her mouth again and now nothing was going to stop him.

As the sun filtered through the curtained window, Avery was still catching her breath while Pete snored softly next to her.

They'd changed everything, more than one time, and now here they were in bed together.

She did this. She made this happen.

Avery slipped out from under his arm and tiptoed to the bathroom.

She shut the door and started the shower. A few moments

later she stepped into the warm stream of water and let it ease the tense muscles in her shoulders and down her back.

Pete loved her.

The words resonated in her head and her chest. *I love you. I've always loved you.*

Wasn't that what everyone kept telling her? The man was in love with her?

Avery slipped her head under the water and let it cascade over her.

She should have known it wasn't just friendship—okay, it was, but she'd always known there was more. A part of her just refused to see it.

Growing up, the girls weren't nice to her. She'd been gangly and skinny, but with her mother's radiant looks. Pete always told her they were jealous.

In high school, it was prestige that came with her background and she let that carry her into bigger social circles.

People were impressed that her father was a doctor and she that came from the Pierponts of Paris, France who had millions in oil fortune.

She wasn't raised like that, but she'd needed the attention. She knew that now.

And through it all who was there? Pete.

Avery pushed back her hair and trembled under the water.

She told him she loved him.

She'd said the very words.

A twinge in her chest had her lifting her hands and pressing them there. She did love him. But she'd never anticipated what happened. This wasn't what she thought would happen—the sex maybe—the love, she wasn't prepared for it.

The tap at the door, before it opened, had her gasping.

"Hey, I would have joined you," Pete's sleepy voice pierced her ears.

"I thought you could use the rest. I'm going to head down to the hospital. I'll be just another moment."

He was silent. That wasn't what he was hoping for, and she knew that.

"I'll make some coffee," he said before the door closed.

Avery let out a breath.

The mistake she had to face wasn't having sex with Pete. It wasn't loving him either. It was knowing that in a few hours she had to tell her parents her plans to move to France. And it was knowing now that she'd faced those feelings for Pete, because she was going to have to let them go.

He didn't deserve her—he deserved better.

It broke her heart to know that while she was away, he'd probably find that better woman and he'd be happy.

PETE HAD DRESSED and gone to the kitchen. He started the coffee and paced. He'd make her some eggs. She liked eggs. Maybe she wanted to go out to breakfast. Perhaps they should just grab drive thru on the way to the hospital.

But he was nearly certain that when she came downstairs, she'd mention that she was going to the hospital alone.

Pete scrubbed his hands over his unshaven cheeks.

What did he really think? Did he think she really loved him? He knew that tone she'd used when he walked into the bathroom. Regret resonated through her words and it stabbed him right in the heart he loved her with.

He pulled a coffee mug from the cupboard and filled it. This was ridiculous. Since they were children they'd been inseparable. They'd fought. They'd made up—of course they'd never taken it as far as they did last night.

He certainly didn't regret it. There would need to be conversation. They needed to discuss this new stage they were in.

One thing that didn't change—he loved her.

The moment he heard her on the stairs, he pulled down another mug and filled it. He'd made it perfectly clear that last night wasn't just for one night. They'd have to work through the doubt. Wasn't that how relationships worked?

"Let's try this morning thing again," he said turning with both mugs in his hands. He handed her one. "Good morning, beautiful."

Pete moved in and brushed a gentle kiss on her lips.

The good thing was she didn't back away. Progress he decided.

"Good morning," she replied with her voice and eyes low.

"I was thinking I'd make some breakfast, or we could go out."

She nodded slightly as she sipped her coffee. "Maybe we can just grab something."

Okay, well, she hadn't said she was going alone. He figured that was two victories.

Pete set his mug on the table, moved in, took hers, and did the same. He pulled her to him, wrapping his arms around her.

"Can I just tell you that any dream I had leading up to last night was squashed. Last night was a dream come true."

She raised her hands to his face and rubbed. "I like this look on you." Her eyes sparkled when she said it, and now Pete was feeling stupid for second guessing what her tone in the shower had been.

"It's no feat for me to be a slob. You just say the word."

She smiled easily now and looked up into his eyes. "In all the years I've known you, you've never been a slob."

"First year of college."

Avery laughed at that. "I take it back."

Pete leaned in and kissed her gently and her lips went pliant and warm under his. Her hands remained on his cheeks and still that explosion of love filled his heart.

"C'mon," he said easing back. "Let's go get some crappy drive thru and head to the hospital." She nodded and let her hands slip from his face and into his hands. "My mom invited us for dinner. I assume with all the babies being born, your family won't be having Sunday dinner tonight?"

She shook her head. "I think Darcy would frown on that today."

He assumed she would. How she still hosted Sunday dinners through her pregnancy was beyond him, but Darcy had done it.

"Mom did comment that she misses you."

Avery smiled as he led her to the door, her hand in his. "It'll be nice to see them before I leave."

Those words were like a knife to his back. His breath had even caught. He promised himself he wouldn't pick a fight, he'd let the comment go.

It had only taken nearly twenty years to make the woman notice him as more than her best friend. He figured it wouldn't take as long to convince her that she needed to stay in Nashville with him and not move to France.

CHAPTER 5

*I*t was no surprise that almost everyone was at the hospital when Avery walked through the door.

Her mother hurried to her the moment she saw her and pulled her to her.

"Clara just went into labor."

Avery stared at her mother. "Really? They're all going to have their babies at nearly the same time?"

Her mother smiled. "It worked for Regan and me." She laughed and wrapped her arm around Avery's shoulders. "Where is Peter?"

Avery loved that her mother always used his full name. It was endearing.

"Parking the car. The lot was full."

Her mother nodded. "Church was in session," she commented about the church just outside of the hospital. "Have you seen Darcy and Ed's little girl yet?"

Avery shook her head. "Pete and I left early this morning." And then ended up in bed together, but she didn't say that aloud. She was sure her mother would know that the moment Pete walked through the door.

"We should go see her. She is beautiful."

Avery let her mother lead her to Darcy's room where Ed sat in a chair by the window, asleep with their other daughter Emily on his shoulder.

Darcy was sitting up in bed holding a little bundle in her arms.

Avery's insides went to mush before she ever peered upon the baby. "Oh, Darcy," she said looking down at her, "she's beautiful."

"Isn't she? She looks just like her daddy."

"Oh, I don't know. I think she looks like you."

"Do you want to hold her?"

Of course she did, but she didn't get to answer. Her mother took the baby from Darcy and turned to hand her to Avery.

She'd held lots of babies over the years, but holding this one, born only hours after her own birthday, seemed to tug at her heart a little more than others.

The door to the room opened and Avery watched as Pete moved in quietly. Before he even looked at the baby, he moved to Darcy's side and kissed her on the cheek.

"How are you feeling?"

"Like a million bucks," she said with a weary smile.

"You look like two million."

Avery swallowed hard. He had a way with the charm and the words. She truly had meant it when she said she loved him.

Pete moved toward Avery. He put his arm around her and looked down at the little bundle she held in her arms.

"What's her name?" he asked and Avery realized she'd never asked.

"Madeline Rae after her grandmothers."

Avery looked up at her cousin. "That is very special."

"They are very special," Darcy added and Avery agreed with a nod.

She looked up at Pete. "Do you want to hold her?"

He only smiled. "You look so good holding her. I think I'll just watch you hold her. Besides, it looks like you'll have another to hold soon."

Darcy leaned forward from her seat in the bed. "Which one?"

"Tori. Madeline said her water finally broke."

Avery felt the tears sting her throat. Little Madeline Rae and her cousin would share a birthday just as she and Spencer did. It was touching.

Pete gave her a gentle squeeze. Obviously, he knew that was sentimental to her.

He looked back at Darcy. "Is there anything I can get for you or Ed? Or little Emily?" he added.

"I think we're doing fine. We've been surrounded by every-one, of course."

"My sisters did everything they could to kick us all out of the hospital. I think they wished they'd have all given birth in other states like Kacey did," Pete said.

Avery thought about it. Kacey's little boy was the only one of Pete's nephews or nieces she hadn't been at the hospital for. They truly had always been together. Why hadn't she ever noticed how intertwined they were? She'd just always expected him to be there.

THEY'D cooed over little Madeline until she was ready to eat. Then they headed back to the waiting room. Avery wasn't too surprised that someone had started a bet on who would have their baby first. The stubborn child of Christian or the anxious child of Clara.

Avery thought her Aunt Madeline radiated, but she had to have been exhausted. She was going to have three grandchildren all born on one day. It was so humorous when Avery thought about it, and she chuckled to herself.

"What's so funny?" Pete gave her a nudge.

"All three of them having their babies on the same day."

"Who wouldn't want to hurry and be here with this family?"

His words were casual, but full of love. He'd always been part of the family. Never had he been awkward when she took him to events or dinners. He just blended in, just as he did now at the hospital surrounded by her family.

Pete let out a long breath. "I'm exhausted. I'm going to go downstairs and get a real cup of coffee. Would you like one?"

She nodded and watched as Pete stood and took orders from anyone who also needed a little shot of caffeine. A few minutes later he was off, with her uncle John in tow.

Her mother slid into the seat Pete had occupied and her aunt Arianna was on the other side. Both women wore eager grins.

"When did this happen?" Her mother asked.

"When did what happen?"

Her mother and aunt exchanged looks as her aunt nudged her. "You and Pete."

"We had almost given up," her mother added.

Avery looked at them. "And you think you know what you're talking about?"

"You are denying it?" her mother asked.

Avery let her shoulders drop. She knew this would happen. Nothing had been different between them. They acted the same as they always did. But there was no lying her way out of this. They'd know and they'd pry until they got the answer they wanted.

"I'm not denying it."

She would have thought it was the announcement of the century the way they both moved in and hugged her in one big group hug.

"I thought you'd blow it," her Aunt Arianna said. "I was afraid he'd meet someone else."

It was all in good humor, but the words hurt. What would she do now if Pete moved on? Yet she planned on moving on.

Nothing was going to stop her from going to France. It was what she wanted.

Perhaps he'd just have to go with her.

PETE AND JOHN put the cups of coffee into the carrying tray. Everyone was dragging. Those who had gone home had only gotten a few hours of sleep. Those who hadn't were working their second day with no sleep.

"How's the job?" John asked Pete as they walked out of the cafeteria.

"It's going well. I'm really building some good portfolios for some clients."

"Sounds good. I know that stock you set up for us is doing well."

Pete laughed. "It should." He pushed the button on the elevator. "I haven't mentioned it to anyone, but I'm up for a promotion."

"And you're mentioning it to me?"

"You're a client. You appreciate my skill."

"That I do," John agreed and stepped into the elevator with Pete as the doors opened. "I guess I'm not the only person that sees your potential then?"

Pete shrugged. "I'm not too optimistic about it. There are some very seasoned professionals that are up for the same promotion."

"Don't discredit yourself. Perhaps your youth will be a benefit for them."

Pete would have liked to think so.

John looked up at the display that counted the floors. "It'll be a good place for you to be in when you and Avery get married."

Pete choked on the air he was breathing when John said that.

"Avery and I are getting married?"

"Aren't you? I mean it's only taken you your entire life to get her."

"Get her? What do you mean get her?"

The door opened and the men stepped out of the elevator and stopped.

"What ever happened last night, it's written all over your faces. No one is judging. We've told her for years you love her. There's never been a doubt she loved you too."

Pete wondered how stupid he looked just standing there staring at John. They all knew? They all knew what they'd done?

He'd never been embarrassed about being around her family, but now since there seemed to be a neon sign on his forehead, he was a little leery about joining in conversation.

John chuckled and gave him a solid pat on the back. "Don't go panicking. You're a part of this family as much as I am. We both had an advantage. We were accepted before we fell in love with the women. It makes for an easier transition."

Pete was sure of that, but how was he supposed to look Simone and Curtis in the eye?

John walked ahead and Pete followed. John passed out the cups of coffee on his tray and Pete tried to keep his composure as he passed out the cups on his tray.

He was only a moment from thinking up an excuse as to why he needed to leave when Madeline appeared in the waiting room smiling a bright smile on a very tired face.

"Clara had a boy! A boy!"

Her husband Carlos moved to her immediately and swung her in a hug. "This is the craziest day ever," he laughed.

Pete's eyes immediately moved to Avery who sat next to her mother wiping happy tears from their eyes.

A set of cousins born on the same day. It was history repeating itself twenty-six years, and one day later.

When she caught his gaze, she smiled and at that moment Pete's heart absolutely melted.

There was something in the way she looked at him that told him she'd heard his plea that last night wasn't the only night. Deep inside, she knew how much he loved her, and he knew that the words she'd spoken were always meant for him as well.

Avery Keller wasn't going to move to France. How could she? Not when they were finally truthful about the love they shared—had always shared.

His mind flashed to her cousins all having babies on the same day and he knew what he wanted.

He was going to marry Avery Keller.

Why wait to ask? It wasn't new, this life they were sharing. They'd been sharing it all along.

His thoughts were interrupted when Christian walked to the waiting room scrubbing his hands over his face.

Immediately his parents went to him. "She's here, but they took her to the NICU."

Madeline reached her hands to his unshaven face. "She's here."

Christian's weary eyes brightened and he smiled. "She's here."

His parents pulled him in to their arms. Pete noticed both Avery and Simone wiping their eyes. Their family had grown today by three.

This wasn't the day to bring up marriage.

He gave it another quick thought. Spencer and Julie hadn't said anything about their assumed engagement.

Pete could wait. For now he'd make her so deliriously happy and in love that she'd never think of leaving Nashville.

CHAPTER 6

*I*n all the years Pete had been spending the night on Avery's couch, or in her spare bedroom, this was the first time she'd ever slept at his place.

The best part about it was she wasn't sleeping on the couch. She was wrapped, skin pressed to skin, with him in his sheets.

He wondered how married couples ever tired of each other. Who wouldn't want to wrap himself around the woman he loved every single night of his life?

Certainly, this was exactly where he always wanted to be.

Avery pressed herself against him and he pulled her in closer. "You do know this is the first night you've ever slept here," he said kissing the top of her head softly.

"That's hard to believe." She let out a sigh. "I guess you were always the gentleman and took me home to tuck me into my own bed."

"It's always nicer to wake in your own bed."

Avery rolled in his arms until she was face to face with him. Her soft breasts pressed against his chest.

Pete pulled the sheets up around them as Avery rested her hand on his cheek.

"I'm grateful for you. I can't imagine my life without you."

Her words resonated in his chest and stirred his heart rate up.

Pete took her hand and kissed her palm. "I don't ever want to think of my life without you."

Avery licked her lips and then pressed them together tightly. "I meant it when I said I love you."

"I meant it when I said it too."

Now he kissed those tight lips, but they didn't go pliant under his as he'd hoped.

Something was occupying her mind and causing her to distance herself, even wrapped in his arms. A moment later the pesky alarm on his cell phone began to buzz and he turned from her to silence it.

"I guess it's back to reality," he groaned.

"Right. Back to work," she confirmed as he wrapped her back in his arms. "I should let you get ready."

"I'll get there." He kissed her softly. "I have time for a shower." He raised his eyebrows. "You might as well get that part of your day out of the way here—with me."

Now she finally smiled. "That would be convenient."

Pete rolled from the bed and tugged her by the hand until she too rolled from the bed and followed him to the shower.

AVERY WAS sure he was going to be late, but Pete insisted on driving her back home. Always the gentleman.

He took her hand in his, lifted it to his lips, and kissed her fingers. "I've been meaning to tell you something. I've been hesitant because I'm a bit pessimistic about it."

"I didn't think you knew how to be pessimistic."

He smiled at that. "Over this I am. I'm up for a promotion."

Avery forced a smile to her face, but happiness for him didn't quite reach her heart. A promotion would mean that he'd be bound to Nashville.

"That's great."

Pete shrugged. "There are two more people, who have more credentials than I do that are up for it too. But if I got it, I'd be in charge of some very significant accounts. It would mean a hefty increase in my income. At twenty-seven, I would be higher up in the company than most people who have been there for decades." His voice rose with excitement.

"That's wonderful."

"Well, like I said, I'm pessimistic. But if they considered me for this promotion maybe I'll be in line for the second—if I don't get it."

She nodded and kept the forced smile. Maybe, if the stars aligned for them, he would in fact get passed up. It might work for her if he didn't get the promotion. He might be more willing to move with her to France, she thought. Time was running out. She'd promised her grandfather she'd be there in a month.

Pete pulled up in front of Avery's house and put the car in park. "I hope you don't mind me not walking you to the door, but…"

"You're late." She pushed open the door. "Thank you for the ride."

Pete reached for her as she began to slide from the seat. "You can't go without a goodbye kiss," he said.

Avery leaned in and let her lips warm under his.

As the kiss lingered, her body hummed. She truly did love this man.

"I'll come by after work. Would you like to go out to dinner? Or I could pick something up."

Avery bit down on her bottom lip. "I'm going to be at Mom and Dad's."

She saw the flash in his eyes, but he smiled through it. "Call me when you get home then."

Avery nodded, climbed from the car, and shut the door. As he drove away she waved and finally let the ache move through her until she cried.

How could she want Pete and the life that was promised to her in France so badly?

CHAPTER 7

a very thought the best way to pass her day would be to pack. She'd received three emails from her grandfather. Every email was filled with photos of the vineyard and the house.

She closed her eyes and thought of the beauty that had greeted her when she'd traveled to France a few weeks ago. Tennessee was beautiful, but France...

She sighed as she thought of it. Wouldn't Pete think it was as lovely too?

Pete.

The thought of him made her heart race. In all her life, his name could bring a smile to her face, but now—it was different.

He loved her. He had told her he loved her.

She loved him too.

Looking back, how had she not known she loved him?

Men had come and gone, but the fact was they'd always gone. She didn't keep them. She didn't want them.

Pete, however, had always been there.

They had celebrated every birthday, Christmas, New Year, and other significant event together for nearly two decades.

Avery was as close to his parents and his siblings as she was to her own parents and her cousins.

Yet, the lure of France tugged at her. The thought of getting to know the part of her family she'd never gotten to know excited her. Perhaps there was more to who she was than she could even imagine.

Her mother was someone else once, and Avery longed to know that life. The luxury, the freedom, the power.

The timer she'd used on her phone chimed and alerted her that it was time to head to her parents' house. It was time to face the changes she was about to make in her life and tell them about her plans.

* * *

Simone Keller had checked her watch before pouring them each a glass of wine and handing Avery's father, Curtis, a beer.

"Never want to be accused of drinking too early," she joked as they all walked out to the patio to sit.

Avery, on the other hand, thought they could use something stronger than wine.

"I put a roast in the oven for dinner. Can you stay?" her mother asked.

"Pete was going to take me to dinner."

Her mother smiled when she mentioned his name, and that in turn made Avery happy. They loved him too.

"That sounds lovely." Her mother sat down in the chair across from Avery and her father sat next to her mother. "So what is it you have come to tell us?"

Her parents exchanged looks and underlying smiles. What did they think she was going to tell them?

Avery took a long sip of her wine and a breath of courage as she lowered her glass.

"I wanted to talk to you about the trip I took a few weeks ago."

Her mother's eyes narrowed and her lips tightened. "The trip to France you neglected to tell anyone about."

"I told Pete."

"You should have told us. You should not have gone in the first place, Avery. You…" Her mother stopped when her father's hand came to her thigh.

"Simone, let her talk."

Her mother let out a huff. "Fine. Talk."

Avery sucked in another courageous breath. "Grandfather has invited me back."

"How generous of him," her mother snapped. "In time you can go back." The angrier she got the deeper her accent became.

"Mom, listen to me. He invited me back because he has the vineyard."

"So? What does he know about vineyards? His business is in oil. That is what he should keep his mind on."

This was going to be harder than she thought. Her mother harbored such hard feelings for Avery's grandfather.

"He wants me to oversee the vineyard and the marketing of the wine."

It grew silent in the backyard of her parents' home. It was as if even the birds were stunned.

Color filled her mother's cheeks. "You will not do that."

"I'm twenty-six years old. I can."

"You will not."

Avery set her glass on the table in front of her so as not to squeeze it too hard and break it.

"I can do this, Mom. I can be what he needs me to be."

"You do not know him."

"You never let me know him."

Now her mother put her glass on the table and inched toward the edge of her seat. "He pushed me away, Avery. His image was more important. I was a pawn in all his games. He turned me away."

"But he came back to see your success. Why can't you be happy for his successes?"

"This vineyard is not a success. It is a buy off."

"For who?"

Her mother looked at her father and then back at her. "For you."

Avery folded her hands tightly in her lap. "Why for me?"

"If you go to France, he wins over me."

Avery dropped her shoulders. "This has nothing to do with you. This has to do with me and my future. He happens to believe in me."

"Curtis, talk to her."

Avery's father set his beer down on the table and turned to her mother instead of her.

"Simone, you have to let her feel this out."

Her mother's eyes grew wide. "You are on her side?"

"I'm not on a side. I just know that she's a lot like you. You're telling her to stay, and she's only going to want to go more."

"I do want to go," Avery interrupted. "Oh, Mom, it's so beautiful there."

"You do not think I know that?"

Avery stood from her chair to kneel down, on the hard cement patio, in front of her mother. "I know you know that. And I also know you think I can do this. But this ridiculous feud between you and Grandfather is what keeps us all apart."

"He disowned me."

"He said he made a mistake."

"But he did it. How do you completely forgive that?" Her mother's hands rose in the air. "How do you excuse that?"

"You don't." Avery took her mother's hands in hers. "You let him in our lives. Let him in a little more."

"I let him in to see what a wonderful woman you were. To prove to him that he was wrong to treat me in such a way."

"Mom, he sees all of that. That's why he offered this opportunity to me. Don't you see that? If you hadn't let him into our lives he wouldn't know what I'm capable of. He'd never have known what you built. Mom, your organization is about helping those who need it. You know what it is to chase a dream and to give back. Well, now it's my turn to chase a dream and give back to all of us. To pull our family together."

Her mother tucked her lip between her teeth in an obvious move to keep it from quivering. "We are a family. We never needed him."

"Mom, I needed both sides of my family. I want this."

Avery's father wrapped his arm around her mother's shoulders. "Simone, give her your blessing."

Her mother shook her head. "I cannot let you go."

"I'm going. Mom, this is an opportunity of a lifetime."

The first tear fell from her mother's eye. "He will betray you."

Avery shook her head. "No, Mom. I don't think he will."

"I'm going to check on the roast," her mother said as she pulled her hands back.

Avery backed up so her mother could stand and walk back to the house.

When she was gone, Avery's father patted the seat where her mother had sat in an offering to her.

Avery took the seat and rested her head against her father's shoulder.

"Are you sure this is what you want to do?" her father asked as he wrapped his arm around her shoulders.

"I do. Oh, Daddy, it's so beautiful there."

"It's beautiful here."

She nodded. "I know." Avery turned to look him in the eye. "I want to try."

Her father kissed her on the head. "You'll do a great job."

This was probably the first time her mother hadn't just agreed with her father. But she understood. She knew her mother would be hesitant.

After a long, quiet moment, her father asked, "What about Pete?"

Avery sank back in the seat and her father was forced to move his arm from around her shoulders and readjust in the chair next to her.

Pete.

She'd thought of him. Of course her father would too.

"I'm going to ask him to go with me," she said softly and then looked up at her father. "Daddy, I love him."

A small smile curled up the corner of his mouth. "I thought maybe you did." Her father patted her hand with his. "You think he'll want to go with you? He has a lot of family here and a good job."

She looked away again and studied the swirls in the cement at her feet. "I'm hoping that I mean more than his job."

Her father sat back in his chair and tilted his head up as if to catch the sun on his face. He didn't have to speak. She knew what he was thinking. Pete had a lot of ties in Nashville. Why would he want to pack up and leave with her without a guarantee of return?

Avery only hoped that maybe he did in fact love her as much as she thought he did. It was all she had to go on.

CHAPTER 8

*D*inner was set on the table and Pete lit the sleek white candles in the center as he watched Avery's car pull up.

Oh, tonight was going to be a night she'd never forget. The day had been glorious and everything was going to be perfect right up until he scooped her off her feet and carried her to bed to make love to her.

He watched her walk from her car, through the yard, up the back steps, and right into the kitchen where he stood.

The candlelight and dinner had caught her off guard, that was obvious by the way she looked at him.

He reached for the two glasses of wine he'd poured and handed her one. "This one is for you, my dear."

Avery took the glass. "What's all this?"

"Dinner."

"You're in a suit," she said grinning.

"I wanted to look nice for you." Pete moved in toward her and kissed her gently, but there was hesitation behind the kiss. He'd thrown her off balance. She'd warm up.

"You cooked and set the table in a suit."

"I plated very fancy carry out, in a suit."

The laugh that had mesmerized him since childhood broke from her and her shoulders eased.

"To be fair, I stole the wine from your reserve too. So I stand before you a great big phony trying to impress you."

Avery moved in closer to him. She trailed her hand up his chest and around his neck. "Peter Grant, you impressed me that day you held your hand out to me on the gravel of the playground when I fell off the monkey bars."

"You wouldn't have fallen off the monkey bars if I hadn't thrown the football at you."

Her lips tightened and her eyes gleamed in contrast. "Are you saying you knocked me down on purpose?"

Pete shrugged his shoulder. "Malcolm wanted to look up your skirt. I didn't want him to do that."

"You risked my life to save my pride?"

"You skinned your knee. It bled for an hour," he reminded her. "I don't think I helped matters much."

Avery moved in until they were tightly pressed together. She rested her forehead against his. "And where is Malcolm now?"

"He owns a telecommunication company. He's worth millions."

Avery laughed, but grew quickly serious again. "I must have gotten over the pain you caused me. I'm right here in your arms."

Pete wrapped his arms around her, careful to keep the glass in his hand upright and not spill it down her back.

"Dinner is ready," the words croaked from his throat as she pressed kisses to it.

"Is it?"

"We should eat."

"Mm-hmm," she moaned against him.

The kisses she was strategically placing on his neck had the blood quickly draining from his head. He moved so he could set his glass down on the table. Pulling back just far enough he took her glass and set it down too.

Avery licked her lips and the very motion had him dragging her back to him to cover her soft mouth with his hungry one.

She gripped him tighter until there was no space between them.

He picked her up and she wound her legs around his waist.

"Microwaves are the greatest invention ever," he said as he carried her to the stairs. "Dinner will wait."

* * *

AVERY RESTED her head against Pete's chest and listened to his heartbeat quicken under her. His breath still came in pants just as hers did.

She hadn't expected him in her house, but she found that she was happy he was there. She was always happier when he was there.

"You had me fooled all this time," he said when his breath had come back to him. "I thought you liked me in my suit."

Avery shifted so that she could look at him. "I do like you in your suit."

A grin moved over his lips. "You sure pulled me out of it fast."

He chuckled and she shook her head as she rested it back against him. "It's hard to believe it took us this long to get to this point, don't you think?"

"The having sex part?"

"Uh-huh."

"You could have convinced me years ago," he said. "I'm glad you came around."

She wouldn't argue that. People had told her for years the man loved her. But even now she was afraid their friendship would never recover if this didn't work out.

Avery rested her chin on Pete's chest. "Dinner looked good. I'm kinda hungry now."

He ran his hand over her hair. "Me too."

"Why did you bring dinner again?"

"I wanted to see you. I knew you'd been to your parents', so I wanted to be here for you. And…" He rolled her onto her back and kissed her long and hard. "I have some things I want to talk to you about."

CHAPTER 9

*P*ete warmed dinner and poured more wine. His slacks were unbuttoned, shirt open, and his feet were bare as he worked in Avery's kitchen.

She sat in a chair in a robe. Her perfectly manicured feet were propped up on the chair next to her and she watched him over the rim of her wine glass.

"I think you're sexy in the kitchen," she said.

"I could do this for you every night, babe."

"Babe?"

"Give me a term. I'll call you whatever."

She sipped her wine and thought. "I always wanted to be a princess."

"You always were mine."

He carried the plates back to the table and she dropped her feet to the floor as she breathed in the scent of the meal.

"It smells as good the second time too."

Pete cut a piece of the chicken from his plate and lifted it on his fork to her lips. She took the bite.

"It tastes good too," she said before finishing the bite and washing it down with a sip of wine.

They ate. She watched him, and he'd reach his hand to her just to touch her.

"Why are you giving me all this attention?" She caught his hand on her knee.

"I told you. All of this wasn't just for one night. I love you, Avery. I always have."

She licked her lips and then bit down on her bottom one. "Pete, something else is going on."

He'd wanted to wait on it, he really had. But after the day he'd had at work, it just wouldn't wait anymore. This was his moment. His grand opportunity.

Since he was a boy he'd followed this gem of a woman around. She was engrained in his family and he in hers. They were friends above all else, and now they were lovers. Oh, and they did that really well too.

But he needed—wanted—more.

He put his fork down and stood from his chair. Reaching for her hand he pulled her up and into his arms. "Let's go into the living room."

"We're not done eating."

"I don't care," he said smiling down at her. "It just can't wait."

Pete led Avery to the living room and sat her down on the couch. He paced for a moment to gather his thoughts. When he knew what he wanted to say, he walked back out to the kitchen to retrieve the box he'd stored in the cupboard.

AVERY SAT on the couch in her white robe. She pushed at her hair and combed her fingers through it as she waited for Pete to stop being so weird. What was he doing tonight? His mind was a million different places.

She'd wanted to be alone tonight just to think things through. They had a lot to talk about.

On the way home from her parents' house she spoke to her grandfather and he was sending a plane for her next the following Wednesday. She had a lot to do before her new life in France started, and now Pete was acting all strange.

She heard him walking back through the kitchen. Straightening up, she placed her hands in her lap and waited.

As he walked into the room he was looking down at a white box with a big red ribbon tied around it.

He was giving her gifts? Her birthday was days ago and he'd given her a very nice Pandora charm for her bracelet. What was he doing now?

He raised his head and those dark brown eyes bore right into her heart.

Pete walked around the table and knelt down in front of her.

"God you're beautiful," he said reaching his hand to her hair.

"Pete, what's going on?"

"I'm admiring you."

Avery swallowed hard. "You're starting to scare me."

He smiled, the gleam in his eyes only getting brighter. "Don't ever be scared of me."

Moving so his body pressed to hers, he wound his hand into her hair and took her under with a kiss. They'd made love already, and yet his kisses could make her head swim.

He lingered his hand on her cheek as he pulled back.

"I wanted to wait on this. I really did." He looked down at the box. "But when your heart knows what it wants—it knows."

He handed her the box.

"What is this?"

Pete chuckled. "You're supposed to open it."

Avery's hands shook as she pulled the tie from the box. When she lifted the lid and saw a ring box inside her heart nearly exploded in her chest.

Pete reached for it and pulled the little box out. "I wanted to wait until the baby buzz wore off the family. And then Spencer could tell everyone about him and Julie."

"They are engaged?"

"I'm still sure they are, aren't you?"

She nodded.

"Anyway, I got to thinking that I've been in love with you all my life. There hasn't been but a few days when I haven't seen your face in all these years. And I'm not sure I've gone a day without talking to you."

"Pete…"

He looked up into her eyes. "I don't want to wait another minute. Avery, will you marry me?"

He pulled open the little ring box. Winking up at her with a sparkle was a solitaire diamond, which must have been at least a carat.

Pete took out the ring and set the box on the table. "I couldn't find a ring that quite mirrored your beauty."

Taking her hand, he held it in his. She felt it shake against his fingers.

Shouldn't she be crying? This was the biggest moment in her life, and she was nearly frozen with fear.

He looked up at her as he poised the ring on the tip of her finger. "I love you. I always have loved you. So what do you say?"

What did she say? Hadn't she spoken? No—no she hadn't. There was only one thing to say. She loved this man more than she'd ever admitted. Perhaps, when she thought about it, it had always been him. Why else hadn't she held on to any of those other men in her life? Now she knew the answer. It was because she was in love with Peter Grant.

"I say yes."

His smile widened and she noticed the tear that shimmered in his eye as he pushed the ring onto her finger.

"I'll make you happy. I promise to always make you happy."

In one quick motion, he'd scooped her under him and laid her back on the couch. His mouth was on hers, taking her breath away.

Mrs. Peter Grant.

Somewhere she'd written that in a notebook. She remembered now. They were going to be married and live happily ever after in France.

CHAPTER 10

*A*very woke in his arms, again. Certainly she'd never tire of that.

She looked down at her finger where the ring he'd put there sparkled. They were getting married.

As much as it was surreal, it felt right. This was where that lifetime of friendship had led them—right into each other's arms.

Once she'd said yes to his proposal, they'd been locked on to each other. They'd made love all night and now woke to the new day—engaged.

Pete's alarm on his phone chimed and he groaned as he rolled to turn it off.

She studied him, rugged from sleep, and she smiled. "Good morning, fiancé."

He hummed and smiled, his eyes nearly closed. "I sure do like the sound of that." He lay there near her for a moment. "I suppose I should get home and get ready. I only had one suit."

"You came to propose and didn't pack a bag?"

Pete gave her a small shrug. "I was too excited to get over here after yesterday. I just didn't think about it."

Avery propped herself up on her elbow. "What was so exciting?" She looked down at her finger. "Okay, the proposal, but you said you'd wanted to wait. Why did you do it last night then?"

Pete rubbed his eyes and sat up, pulling her up with him.

Avery turned to him, covering her body with the sheet for modesty sake.

"Aside from not wanting to spend another moment without you," he said raising his hand to her cheek. "I got some great news yesterday and I knew the moment was right."

Avery smiled. "What news?"

Pete lifted his chest and pushed back his shoulders. "I got the promotion."

She opened her mouth to congratulate him before her mind spun it around.

He got the job. The very job she was banking on him not getting.

She let out the breath she was holding. "Congratulations."

Pete studied her for a moment. His own smile faded away. "You don't sound very genuine."

Avery lifted her chin. "Of course I am. You deserve it."

Pete's eyes narrowed. "You're using that debutante bullshit on me. C'mon, tell me what you really think."

Avery swung her legs over the side of the bed, taking the sheet wrapped around her with her as she stood. "I forgot. I was going to go to a yoga class this morning. I should..."

Pete swiftly moved from the bed and stood in front of her, his naked body uncovered.

"This isn't what I was expecting. Why aren't you happy for me?"

Those tears she'd expected last night were now battling to surface. "I am happy for you. You deserve this."

"You said that."

"Well, it's true."

He moved closer to her and took her arms in his hands. "You're running. Don't run from me."

She pulled from his grip. "Fine. I didn't want you to get the job."

Disappointment washed over his face breaking her heart into a million pieces.

"You didn't want me to get the job I've been working my ass off for? Well, that's supportive of you."

"Pete, it's not that you shouldn't have gotten it. I just was hoping maybe you'd be up for it again—later."

He took a step toward her forcing her to take a step back. "Why didn't you want me to have that job? You have something else you want to say."

It shouldn't be this hard, she thought. Of course, she had something to say. Had he forgotten her plans?

"I wanted you to move to France with me."

Pete deflated right in front of her. He turned and scrubbed his hands over his face. "You wanted me to pick up my life and just move away?"

"With me," she pleaded.

"With you? Avery, why are you even considering going? You don't know that man at all."

"He's my grandfather," she said trying to catch her breath.

"Right. And you've only seen him a handful of times in your entire life. Now he offers you something you know nothing about and you're willing to leave your entire family and move to a country you've only visited? I don't think you know what you're doing."

"I thought you supported me."

"I do support you. I think you can do amazing things. I don't happen to share the same enthusiasm in you doing those things in France where you'll have no one."

"I'll have my grandfather."

Pete nodded sarcastically. "Right. That worked out so well for your mother."

Avery just stared at him. "You won't go with me?"

"Avery, we just decided to get married. We can't just run off and live somewhere else."

"Yes we can."

Pete turned and picked up his pants from the floor and slipped them on. "I have to go to work. We can talk about this tonight."

"I leave next Wednesday."

Pete buckled his belt and reached for his shirt. "We will talk about it tonight," he said again.

Avery felt her heart shatter. "I leave next Wednesday."

Pete lifted his head. "You're moving to France? That's the end of it? No discussion? No talking it over with me? You're just going."

"I leave next Wednesday," she repeated as her heart slammed in her chest.

He pursed his lips, picked up his suit jacket, and draped it over his arm. "I just got a huge promotion. I passed over two senior investors. I've worked my ass off for the past three years for this. Next Wednesday I'll still be here."

Without another word, he walked past her and out of the house.

CHAPTER 11

One day had become two—then three. Pete hadn't called. He hadn't come by the house, texted, or even emailed. He'd simply walked out of the bedroom that morning and never looked back.

Avery looked down at her phone screen. The text message she had sent him an hour ago was marked read. She was reaching out to him and he wasn't responding.

How could he simply think that walking away would be better?

She looked at the ring on her finger. It sparkled as brilliantly as it had the other night, but it hurt to look at it.

Avery made her way around boxes, which filled the living room, to the kitchen for another cup of coffee. She hadn't slept in three nights.

Had he seen her drive by his house? Did he ignore the doorbell when she'd rung it?

At least when she'd called his office yesterday they told her he was in a meeting, so she knew he was alive and well—and avoiding her.

Her mother, thank goodness, had called her and apologized

for her breakdown. She made it clear that though she wasn't thrilled with Avery's decision, she'd stand behind her. Then she proceeded to invite her to dinner on Sunday.

Avery graciously accepted. It would be her last family dinner before her new journey—alone—began.

SHE MUDDLED THROUGH ANOTHER DAY, and by Friday afternoon she was all packed and waiting for the shipping company to come and take her things. They'd promised to be there by three and it was already four.

It would be an easy move. Nothing but clothes and necessities. The furniture belonged to the house—the house where almost all the Kellers and Bensons had lived on their journey into adulthood.

When the doorbell rang she moved to the door. Once they loaded up her boxes what else would she do with her weekend?

Avery opened the door expecting some man in a bland uniform and a wheeler, instead Pete stood before her.

His hair was in need of a trim and he certainly needed to shave. The week had left its tracks on him as well.

"Pete…"

"I know you didn't expect me. I just…"

She took his hand and pulled him inside before she lunged at him and wrapped her arms around his neck. It took a moment before he gathered his arms around her and held her.

But his hold didn't feel right. None of it felt right.

Pete stepped back and shoved his hands into his pockets. "I wanted to apologize."

"I understand. I don't blame you for walking out."

He ran his tongue over his teeth. "I didn't mean about walking out."

"Oh." What could he mean she wondered? After all, he'd just

up and left. Then ignored her. She'd never gone nearly a week without talking to him.

"Hundreds of times I've dropped you off and tucked you in. I've slept in that guest room and on that couch more times than I'd like to have counted. I should have done that when I brought you home after your birthday. I should have kissed your cheek and gone home."

Avery fisted her hands on her hips. "You're sorry for what we did?"

He nodded. "If I had just gone home, our friendship would be in tact, and I'd be only heartbroken because I wouldn't see you everyday while you lived in France. I'd go to visit. Drink wine. Maybe meet some French girl."

That one stung, she thought as he took a breath to continue.

"I wouldn't have poured my freaking soul out to you and proposed had I just walked out that night."

The tears that were fighting to get to her eyes stung in the back of her throat. "You regret proposing?"

"It didn't do me any damn good did it?"

"In case you forgot, I said I'd marry you."

"And then turned right around and told me you wished I hadn't gotten my promotion because you're moving to France."

Avery moved toward him, but Pete took a step back. Heat from the anger pulsing through her warmed her skin. "I want this, Pete. I want this as much as I want to marry you."

He shook his head. "I didn't think you were as shallow as you've proven to me that you are."

"Exactly what does that mean?"

"You want to move away as much as you want to marry me. Honey, when you love someone you're usually willing to make sacrifices."

She crossed her arms. "What about you? You don't love me enough to make sacrifices for me?"

"Is that what you think?"

"You chose your job."

He stepped closer to her and narrowed his dark, angry eyes at her. "I quit my job yesterday."

AND THAT, Pete thought, was the reaction he'd hoped for. Avery's eyes were wide and her mouth hung open. She, for the first time in as long as he could remember, was speechless.

"You quit your job for me?"

"For us," he corrected.

"But your promotion..."

Pete shrugged. "I love you more."

She lifted her hands to her mouth and the sobs came quickly. He wanted to scoop her up, but there was still some invisible wall between them.

"You quit your job to move to France with me? To marry me?"

Now he stepped in, though the air was still thick between them. He gathered her hands in his. "Avery, for as long as I can remember, you're all I've ever wanted. I was willing to forgo the thought that someday that might happen. I cherished our friendship more. But you said you loved me and you said you'd marry me. So, yes. I quit my job, passed up my promotion, and am willing to leave my family behind to follow you."

She let out a long ragged breath. "That's a lot of responsibility."

"You're willing to leave your family for this. That means it's very important to you. It means you think this is what you need to do. The Avery Keller I know doesn't take lightly the commitment of family."

A line formed between her brows. "Right."

"I need to go home and pack and get things settled in my world."

"I'll come with you," she offered, and he shook his head.

"I need some time to process this."

Avery stepped back from him. "My parents want me over for dinner on Sunday. I assume it won't just be my parents."

"Usually, with your family, that's how it works."

"Will you come? We can share our news."

Pete nodded. "I'll be there."

He moved in and pressed a kiss to her forehead. "I'll come by in the morning."

He took his keys from his pocket and headed toward the door.

"Pete," she called after him and he turned to look at her. "I love you."

He smiled, but it felt forced. He gave her a nod and walked out. At that very moment he needed to save his *I love you too* until he didn't feel jaded about it.

CHAPTER 12

*P*ete sat in his bedroom with his suitcase open to the side of him. It was empty. He was empty.

He lowered his head into his hands. Avery Keller was going to be his wife. The thought lightened the pain going through him. She said she loved him and she was going to marry him—Avery.

He'd never told her that once he'd even written their names together and named all their children. It had been a childish dream back then, but now it was real.

What the hell did it matter that he'd given up his apartment and his job? Those weren't his identity. But being Avery's husband would be.

The pain in his chest seemed to ease.

He stood and walked to the dresser. Pulling out the contents, he placed them in the suitcase. There was an ease to the packing now.

Next week he was going to be living in France on a vineyard.

A smile actually came to his lips. He could even see Avery, her dark French beauty with the beautiful vineyard backdrop.

He didn't speak French. Was that going to be a problem?

It was something to consider. He needed to learn it, but when he came back to Nashville, he'd speak French.

Where would they travel when they were there, he wondered as he emptied another drawer. It was the opportunity to see the world with the woman he'd loved since he was just a little boy.

*　*　*

AVERY HAD MANAGED an eye open to look at the clock. It was seven o'clock and she was sure she'd heard the back door open.

If it wasn't for the fact that every person she knew had a key, she'd probably have jumped out of bed, grabbed the baseball bat from under her bed, and headed down to check it out.

Whoever had come in the door had dropped their keys, noisily, on the counter. Now they were whistling.

Avery rolled over and looked at the bedroom doorway. She recognized the song before she did the whistle. *My Girl*, brought a smile to her face.

A moment later Pete was leaned up against her doorjamb with a cup of coffee in his hand.

"Vanilla latte?" she asked, her voice cracking under protest.

"Anything for my princess," he said moving toward her.

Avery sat up in the bed and took the paper cup with the cardboard sleeve on it. "You're much earlier than I thought you'd be."

Pete sat down on the bed next to her and she inhaled his fresh cologne—savoring its comfort.

"I had a change in attitude last night, and I couldn't wait to get here."

"You could have come back last night."

Pete lifted his own cup to his lips and took a careful sip. "I needed to make sure I let all the anger go."

Avery reached out for him and he took her hand. "I didn't mean to make you mad about it all."

"Give and take. That's what makes a relationship. Avery, I

meant it that night. Never for one night. I knew already I wanted forever. And this is only going to be one of the misunderstandings we have between us. There are going to be many more of them."

"Thank you. I know what this is costing you."

Pete leaned in and kissed her gently. "You can make it up to me. I want our daughter to be named Mildred."

Avery crinkled up her nose. "You're right. We're going to have many more arguments."

"Mildred is out?"

"It's hideous."

"It's my grandmother's."

Avery held back her smile. "It might make a wonderful middle name."

Pete gave her leg a pat. "Give and take. You're beginning to get the concept."

CHAPTER 13

*W*ith all of her belongings gone, Avery was living out of a suitcase. It was decided, between both of them, that she'd live at Pete's until Wednesday. The shipping company would pick up his belongings on Tuesday. Then they would set out on a journey of a lifetime together. They'd move to France and plan their wedding. They'd start their new life, and learn to be their own family. They'd have each other.

Sunday afternoon, as they drove down the street where her parents lived, she laughed when she saw the cars lined up.

"I told you it wasn't going to be just a dinner."

"Avery, I've been around this family long enough to know how it works. What I didn't tell you was my folks want us for dinner tomorrow night. You're going to have the same thing."

She liked that. It was one thing they certainly had in common—a large family. Never had Avery felt as if she were really an only child. How could she? Sure, the dynamics between her and her cousins was a little different than that of Pete and his brothers and sisters. But a close family was a close family.

Pete found a parking place nearly a block from her parents'

house. He parked, turned off the car, and sat quietly for a moment.

"Is something wrong?" Avery asked.

Pete shook his head and then lifted it to look at her. "It's going to be strange, living away from everyone, isn't it? No big Sunday dinners at your family's or mine. No late nights at the hospital with new babies arriving all at one time," he said with a chuckle.

"Are you having second thoughts?"

Pete shook his head. "No. I was just thinking it would be different. Not impossible."

They climbed from the car and walked hand in hand to her parents' front door. Darcy was just inside bouncing a crying Emily and trying to soothe her.

"Is she okay?" Avery asked as they walked into the house.

"I think she has a little tummy ache. Ed is on a phone call. I need to nurse the baby, but she won't stop, and won't let me put her down," Darcy said in a frazzled, lack of sleep voice.

Pete instinctively reached out. "Let me see if this helps." He took Emily from her mother and rested her on his wide shoulder. A few sobs later and Emily calmed.

"What did you do?" Darcy asked.

"I'm just built right for correct pressure on babies' tummies. I could always get my nieces and nephews to calm this way." Emily gave a few more big gasps from her sobs and soon was asleep on Pete's broad shoulder. "Go feed the baby. She's fine with me."

Darcy kissed him on the cheek, and then looked at Avery. "He's a gem. You should catch him before someone else does," she said as she moved into the house in search of her baby.

"It's a good thing you caught me," he joked. "I seem to be perfect."

"She didn't say that."

"Yes she did. Don't mess with my ego. I'll wake Emily up and hand her to you."

Avery thought the threat wasn't worth it. She kissed him on

the cheek and they walked into the house where her family all waited for her.

Everyone one but Christian and Victoria were there. Their daughter was still in the NICU, but her aunt Madeline assured Avery that she was growing by leaps and bounds.

"A few more days until she's big enough to move home with her parents and her cousins," Madeline said.

Avery was happy for them. They were raising Victoria's niece and nephew. They'd lost their first baby, and now their daughter was still in the hospital. They were truly a family that proved that love could triumph over all.

Avery's mother stood in the kitchen, a glass of wine in her hand and a tissue in the other.

"Is everything okay?" Avery asked her.

"I miss you already and you haven't left."

Avery pulled her into her arms and held her. "Just think. It'll be the most wonderful reason for you to visit me in France."

Her mother nodded. "I know. My mother has been begging me to do that for years, and I am sure my father would be cordial enough."

"He loves you, Mom."

"I know. Avery, you will just never understand."

No, she was sure she wouldn't. But she also couldn't imagine her grandfather was the same man that banished her mother when she'd become pregnant. However, he'd been nothing but gracious to Avery. She was willing to move across the world to take what he was offering. Avery figured she needed to give the man the benefit of the doubt.

"How come you're always the last one to the party?" Spencer walked into the kitchen and swept Avery up into a grand hug.

"I didn't know I was late."

"You're always late, now come out here." He gave her arm a tug and pulled her to the living room where Spencer had obviously gathered everyone.

Avery moved in next to Pete as Spencer put his arm around Julie.

"This has got to have been the longest week of my entire life," he began. "Most of you have busted my chops about missing half of my birthday party last week because I ducked out. Fine. I did." Julie nudged him with a grin. "And then what was with all the babies trying to get in on mine and Avery's birthday?"

The family laughed and Avery smiled lovingly at her cousin. She hoped the cousins born the day after their birthday would share the same special bond that they did.

Spencer kissed Julie on top of her head. "The reason I left early that night was to avoid a black and pink birthday cake."

Again, the family laughed and Avery coughed behind a disguised, "You're welcome."

"But I had something very important to attend to. Julie agreed that night to be my wife."

Avery was sure that the announcement wasn't a surprise to any of them, but they all cheered and moved in around the couple to congratulate them and honor them.

When Avery made it to Spencer she cupped his face in her hands and gave him a noisy kiss on the cheek. "I will always make you celebrate with a pink and black cake. In fact, I want to be in charge of your wedding cake."

"No," he said pulling her hands from his face and then looked down at her ring.

Julie looked down as Spencer brought Avery's hand into view.

"What is this?" he asked and the sparkle had left his eyes.

She'd forgotten she'd had it on. Perhaps she should have taken it off.

Pete moved in behind her and Spencer lifted his eyes to him. "Are you kidding me?" he whispered.

"About what?" Pete asked as he wrapped his arms around Avery's waist.

Spencer leaned in. "What's going on?" He was still whispering.

"I caught her, Spence. I'm getting a wife too."

"No shit!" There was no whispering now as Spencer leaned back and Julie pushed in to hug Avery.

Darcy moved in next to her brother. "What?"

Spencer lifted Avery's hand and showed it to Darcy.

"What is that? That's a ring! What are you wearing a ring for? Who?" she asked as she looked at Pete. "You and Pete? When did this happen? Where have I been?"

Her voice had risen too and soon Avery's parents had made their way to the center of the crowd.

"Avery?" Her father looked at her.

Avery looked up at Pete who winced. "Well, this isn't how I expected this to go." He rubbed the back of his neck with his hand. "Sir, it seems as though in my excitement, I missed a step."

"You missed a step? Maybe you should fill me in." Her father's eyebrows raised.

Avery looked around at her family, which had all gathered in close. She was sweating, and she was sure that Pete was too.

"Mr. Keller, without your blessing, I asked your daughter to marry me. But right now, I sure would like your blessing."

Her father continued to stare at him a moment too long, Avery thought, before a smile moved across his lips.

"I have no idea how you finally convinced her, but son, you're the only man I ever would have given my blessing to."

Her father pulled Pete to him first, before he included her in their embrace. A moment later the entire family was congratulating them.

When Spencer finally gathered her in his arms, she whispered in his ear. "I'm sorry. That was supposed to be your moment."

"I figure we now know why we were all here."

"I thought you were here to see me off."

He pushed back and looked down at her. "See you off. You're still not thinking of moving are you? That's ridiculous."

"Avery?" Her mother's voice broke through the noise of the

celebration and she looked at her. "You're getting married, and you're still moving?"

Could she possibly break the woman's heart any more than she was?

Pete stepped to her side. "Mrs. Keller, Avery really feels strongly about going to France. I'll be there to take care of her. I promise."

Her mother looked at Pete. "I heard you were up for a promotion. You didn't get it?"

Pete looked down at Avery, and gave her a reassuring squeeze as he wrapped his arm around her shoulder.

"I did get the promotion. I gave it up to be with Avery. I love her. I have always loved her."

Tears streamed down her mother's cheeks. "I knew that part. I'm going to miss the two of you." She pulled them in and held them as she cried.

Avery let her own tears fall. There were no more secrets, she thought. They could get on that plane on Wednesday and fly away—together.

CHAPTER 14

*P*ete thought he should have been enjoying a day where he wasn't at work, but it only managed to remind him that he didn't have a job.

The landlord had dropped by and they had made arrangements for Wednesday's departure. He was sad to see Pete go, he'd said. It seemed that Pete was an ideal tenant. The new tenant would be moving in on Thursday.

As they readied to go to his parents' house for dinner he noticed that Avery had nearly been avoiding him.

Standing in front of the bathroom mirror he watched as she pulled her long, beautiful hair back and banded it into a ponytail.

She looked into the mirror and batted her eyes at him. "What are you looking at?"

"You. You're just the most beautiful woman I've ever seen."

She turned, moved to him, and wrapped her arms around his neck. "I'm nervous. What if your mom cries like mine did?"

Pete pulled her in. "She will. Just be ready for it. I have sisters too. They're going to cry."

"I feel horrible. I'm taking you away from them."

"I made my own choice. Besides, by the time they're done

being shocked that I finally convinced you to marry me, they won't notice we're in France."

She focused those dark chocolate eyes on his. "Pete, you've always been my dearest friend. And I won't lie, I thought about us a few times, but I thought you only loved me as your friend. When did you decide I was the one?"

He tried to control his grin, but it pushed through. "About the seventh grade."

"No," she laughed. "Be serious."

Pete lifted her chin with his finger. "I've never been more serious."

He wondered how she never could have known how he felt. Surely he hadn't been able to hide it as hard as he tried. Obviously he hadn't done too well. The entire Keller family knew how he felt about her, and how many times had his sisters and his mother asked when he was going to finally make his move on her?

"Do you think your mother will be okay with me? I mean as a daughter-in-law."

"Avery she loves you as much as she loves my sisters."

She rested her head against his chest. "I love them, Pete. I just want them to be happy."

Because he knew his own voice wouldn't be steady enough to convey it, he didn't tell her they'd be fine with it. His mother and father adored and loved Avery. However, deep inside he knew that his mother would have reservations about them moving, though she'd never think about sharing them in front of Avery.

Avery stared at the overfilled plate in front of her. As usual Pete's mother had over done herself. On short notice, only his sister Kacey and his brother Sean, and their families, had made it to dinner. That was all the better, Avery thought. The moment Kacey had seen her ring, she'd started to cry. Then his mother cried. Sean's wife cried, and that sent his daughter into hysterics because everyone else was crying.

Avery did have her confirmation on how much his mother cared for her though. She'd immediately pulled to her bosom and held her there for a long time. Then she hurried her through the house to show Avery her well-preserved dress and her wedding album.

It was a bonding moment for the women. No longer was Avery just Pete's best friend, and the woman he took care of. She was to be his wife, and it seemed as though that thought made his mother very happy.

"I should have lunch with your mother," Pete's mother said as she turned the page to her wedding album. "I haven't had the pleasure for years."

"She'd enjoy that. She loves to lunch," Avery laughed. "I suppose that stems from her old life."

"I wondered if she ever missed that jet set life."

Avery had always assumed she missed it a little bit. The trade off, however, had been greater. True love was abundant around Avery. She'd seen it in her parents, her grandparents, and her aunts and uncles. Now her cousins had all married, and they were absolutely all smitten with their husbands and wives—just as she was finding she'd been with Pete for years. Well, she was known for being stubborn. She figured having taken so long to realize she was in love with the man proved it.

"Do you suppose you'll honeymoon somewhere?" his mother asked as she pulled a photo album out of the chest where she'd collected so many memories.

"I've never been to Monte Carlo."

His mother's eyes widened. "Oh, I think of Grace Kelley when I think of Monte Carlo. She was such a beautiful bride, and don't you think Kate Middleton's dress was just as classy? What kind of dress are you thinking of?"

Avery didn't know what to say. She hadn't really thought

about anything that had to deal with the wedding. She was just thinking about getting on that plane Wednesday morning and having Pete right next to her.

"I don't know. But knowing my mother's love for fashion I'm sure..."

Both women turned their heads toward the door when they heard something crash to the floor in the other room. Before they could get to their feet, she heard Pete's voice yell, "Dad!"

CHAPTER 15

*P*ete fell to the floor next to his father. One second he'd been putting a covered dish in the refrigerator, and the next moment he was grabbing hold of the shelf and then falling to the ground, taking the shelf full of items with him.

Quickly, Pete pushed away everything that had fallen around his father as his sister fell to the floor next to them. Her husband grabbed for their children and escorted them out of the room.

"Avery!" Pete shouted. "We need you!"

"We need to call 911," Kacey said as she stared at their father.

Pete shot her a look. "Do it!"

Avery and his mother skirted the wall into the kitchen at the same time. Avery dropped down right next to him as her father had trained her to do. His mother gripped the counter, and his brother moved in and steadied her.

Pete watched Avery assess his father while he heard his sister on the phone.

"What happened?" she asked, her voice calm and stern.

"He just collapsed."

Avery placed her hands on his father's shoulders and shook

him as if to wake him. "Mr. Grant, are you ok?" she shouted at him.

There was no response.

She checked his pulse and then lowered her ear to his nose and mouth.

"He's not breathing. We need to do CPR. Do you remember how to do this?" She looked at him as she positioned herself above his father.

Pete nodded. Curtis had given multiple classes on CPR, and he'd demanded Avery be at every one of them. Pete had been to a few, but under her direction, he knew she could walk him through it.

He looked up at his mother who was as white as a ghost.

Avery averted her attention to her as well. "Mrs. Grant, I'm going to start CPR. Kacey is calling for an ambulance. Perhaps you can let them in. Gather his identification and anything he might need."

His mother nodded, and Pete knew it was as much a tactic to keep her calm as it was to get her out of the room.

Swiftly, Avery moved into position. "I'm going to do compressions. You're going to do breaths."

He watched as she placed one hand over the other and interlaced her fingers. Placing them on his father's chest, her elbows stiff, she began to administer compressions. She counted each one.

Pete positioned himself next to his father's head. When Avery gave him the signal he pressed his hand to his father's forehead, tilting his father's head back, and opening his airway.

"Check for breath," she reminded him.

He listened, but there was nothing. She gave him a nod and Pete administered the first of two breaths, watching his father's chest rise as he did so. Then he gave another breath.

Avery checked for a pulse, but when she shook her head she began compressions again.

Pete felt as though the process had gone on for hours, but it was a mere four minutes before he heard the sirens from a fire truck followed by the ambulance.

Soon they were spectators as the professionals stabilized his father and pushed him out of the house and into the ambulance.

Pete's mother had gathered all the items Avery had told her to, and she rushed out with him.

"You all go, I'll stay with the kids," Avery said, as Kacey, Sean, and their spouses seemed to stand frozen watching the commotion.

Kacey gave her a nod. "Thank you," she said, sobbing now.

Avery looked toward Pete. "Go with them. Keep me informed."

She still hadn't broken. Fully in control she reached for his hand and gave it a squeeze. "He needs you with him."

Pete could feel his muscles begin to shake. On this evening of celebration, he and Avery had just saved his father's life. Oh, who was he kidding? Her level head, her strong will, her preparedness had saved his father.

Now here she was taking care of what needed to be taken care of so he could be with his family.

Indeed, he loved this woman to the moon and back.

Pete moved to her, gathered her in his arms, and placed a kiss against her lips. "I love you. Thank you."

She gave him a gentle smile. "Go. He needs you."

Pete nodded, and a moment later, was piling into his car with his sister, brother, and their spouses as Avery stayed behind to care for his nieces and nephews.

AVERY GATHERED the kids around the TV and found them a movie to watch. Luckily there had been a Frozen DVD. That seemed to capture their attention.

When they were all calmly watching the movie, she made

them a snack, and then sat just out of earshot and called her mother.

The moment she heard her mother's voice, her strength crumbled.

"Avery, what is it, darling? What is wrong?" Her mother's voice rose in pitch.

Avery gripped the phone trying to keep her hand from shaking.

"Mom, I need you. Can you please come over to the Grants'?"

"Is everything alright?"

Avery shook her head and closed her eyes trying to hold in the tears so they wouldn't fall. She was losing the battle. "Pete's father had a heart attack."

She heard her mother gasp. "Oh, Avery."

"Pete and I did CPR. They're all at the hospital now, but, Mom," the tears finally burst through. "I need you."

"I will be there as quickly as I can," she promised and then the phone went quiet.

Avery went to the bathroom and cleaned herself up. The kids didn't seem to be shaken, and she wasn't going to rattle them by crying. Though the moment her mother walked through the door, she couldn't promise herself she wouldn't break down.

MACHINES BEEPED and another machine pushed air into Pete's father's lungs. Even in a dimly lit, quiet room, it was noisy.

His mother sat holding his father's hand, and he sat at the foot of the bed trying to keep from falling asleep.

The doctor said that the chances of a full recovery were good since Pete and Avery had jumped so quickly to save his father's life. Pete couldn't take the praise though. It was all Avery.

Once again, he was watching another morning arrive in a

hospital. If his mother had wanted to go home, he'd have taken her. But she wanted to be by his father's side.

In time, she'd have to go, but for now, he'd appease her and he'd stay with her.

He'd sent his sister home in his car. His brother was in the waiting room sleeping with his feet propped up on a chair.

Once his father had been admitted, he'd called Avery. Though her voice was as steady as she'd been when she'd sent him away, he knew she'd broken down. After all, she'd told him her mother was there with her.

Pete rested his head back against the wall. Things had changed when his father fell to the ground. Not only had Pete's own life flashed before his eyes as he watched him, but all plans were off now. There was no way he could go to France. Avery was going to have to call her grandfather and let him know that she wouldn't be moving.

CHAPTER 16

*A*very had her mother take her back to Pete's when his sister had arrived to relieve her. She was exhausted, and the moment she fell into the bed, she was swiftly taken by sleep.

She woke to soft kisses on her cheek, and sunlight was to peeking through the curtains.

"Pete," her voice was still full of sleep as she sat up next to him.

His face was shadowed by a day's worth of whiskers, and his eyes were darkened with circles from lack of sleep.

"Your dad?"

Pete let out a deep sigh. "He'll recover. He has a long road ahead of him, but he's alive."

Avery reached toward him and pulled him to her. He clung to her, holding her tightly, and sobbing.

She wasn't sure how long she held him in her arms, but when she felt her arms go numb, and his body grew heavy, she shifted.

"You need to lie down and get some sleep."

Pete nodded.

Avery moved so that he could lie in the bed where she had

slept. She noticed the clock on the nightstand. It was six o'clock. For a moment, she considered curling up next to him, but it wasn't but a moment later and he was fast asleep. She'd let him be. She had emails to answer and phone calls to make. There was so much to do before tomorrow morning.

PETE FOUND Avery hunched over her laptop with a half eaten sandwich on a plate next to her. She had a notepad next to her and was jotting down something she'd looked up on the internet.

He moved to her and rested his hands on her shoulders.

Avery jumped. He'd startled her.

"Sorry," he said softly as he kissed the top of her head.

"I was absorbed."

Pete sat down in the chair next to her. "What are you studying?" he asked as he picked up the paper next to her. "These are kinds of wine grapes."

"Right. I figured if I went in with a little knowledge, Grandfather would be impressed."

Pete dropped the notebook on the table. "It'll all have to wait, Avery. We can't go now."

Her eyes open wide and her lips parted. "Excuse me?"

"My father is going to be in the hospital for a while. They're talking surgery. That means recovery. He needs me right now and we're just going to have to wait on this trip to France."

"Trip to France? This isn't just a trip."

Pete gritted his teeth. "Regardless of what you're calling it, I can't go to France right now. My family needs me here and damn it, Avery, you're part of that family."

"All of my belongings are there. Pete, I've set up everything to leave on Wednesday."

He shoved his chair back and stood to pace the kitchen. Everything inside of him wanted to explode. What was she thinking? Was she seriously considering going to France when he was in the middle of all this? This whole plan to move to France was ridiculous anyway. Avery had lost her damned mind.

"I have savings. We can get your stuff shipped back here. We'll have to move into your place. This one is…"

Avery pushed back her chair and stood erect. She pushed her shoulders back and tossed that long dark hair behind her. She was gearing for a fight and Pete was ready. She'd made all the decisions their entire life. It was time for her to understand that his decisions meant something too.

"My grandfather already has a plane coming for us."

"Then I guess we'll have to pay him back for his lost expenses."

The color in her cheeks reddened. "I'm leaving on that plane in the morning, Pete."

"And when did you become so selfish?"

"Selfish? I planned on this long before you decided we should get married."

"Me?" Oh, now he was furious. He moved swiftly toward her, stopping before he grabbed her arms. "Are you not part of this relationship? Are you telling me you didn't want to marry me?"

Her shoulders dropped and so did her gaze. "No. I didn't mean that."

"Avery, I gave up everything to move with you and marry you. Don't you think you could give me a little consideration when it comes what I need?"

She moved in and wrapped her arms around him. "I'm sorry. I'm so sorry."

Pete gathered her in his arms. "Without you he wouldn't still be here," he said. "You saved my father's life."

"I did what I'm trained to do."

There was more to it than that. He knew it.

A great deal of tension still brewed between them. In the

morning, all decisions would be final. A twist in his gut told him he needed to be prepared for the moment she stepped on that plane and flew away—forever.

CHAPTER 17

$\mathcal{A}$very had paced every inch of Pete's house. He'd taken his mother back to the hospital and Avery had refused to go.

Her heart was breaking, and there were moments she'd thought she could actually die from the pain.

No one in her life made her feel the way Pete made her feel. It was no wonder she'd kept him by her side for so long. She loved him. She truly loved him.

But a part of her had to go.

Her entire life, she'd absorbed all the stories of her mother's life before she'd run off with her father. There were parties all over the world. She'd known princes and kings. There were clothes, cars, and a lavish life that Avery wanted to taste and to feel.

Everything about her screamed Parisian debutante. She looked like her mother, and her mother had trained her to be accepted in every social circumstance.

Being the daughter of a well-respected doctor had given her some fine lineage to work with in Nashville. Her mother had also kept many of her high-class friends. So Avery was no stranger to what could be.

Maybe Pete was right. Maybe she was a little selfish, but she needed to be. She didn't have musical talent like Clara or a physical talent like Christian. She couldn't design and build buildings like Ed and Spencer. Her mother had raised her to give back and to fundraise for charity, but it was her cousin Tyler that thrived at that. Avery was good at nothing.

Her grandfather thought she had some potential though. He was willing to bet a lot on it too. Wouldn't it be a waste if she didn't go? What if it was her calling in life? What if she belonged in France?

Love should make her stay in Nashville, she thought as she fixed the pillows on the couch before plopping down on them. Love should make France dull in comparison to what could be if she stayed.

It had been a longing of hers longer than wanting marriage, a house, and a family of her own. There was a wanderlust burning inside of her. She ached to be someone—and to be more than just Pete's someone.

The thought, though empowering, shattered her. If she walked away, she'd lose him. Lover or not, he was her best friend. Would he be that again? Would she want him to be?

Her chest ached and she could taste the tears before they began to stream down her cheeks.

Avery owed this moment of self-discovery to herself. Chances were she'd know right away if moving to France was right. Pete had always been there to see her fly and to catch her when she fell. He'd be there again—right? There was no reason to think differently.

Pete could stay in Nashville, and see to his father.

Avery could go to France, and see if it settled her.

It wouldn't be forever that they'd have to be apart. Soon they could be in each other's arms again when he felt as though he could leave his father's side.

She looked down at the ring on her finger and gave it a twist. Pulling it from her finger, she looked it over. It was the right thing to do, she decided as she set it on the coffee table. Someday they'd laugh over it. It would be a story to tell their grandchildren about.

Through the tears, she managed to get up and find a piece of paper in a packed box by the door. She wrote him a letter and left it under the ring. In less than twelve hours, she'd be on a plane. This was for her. Selfish as it did seem, just like he said it was, it was for her.

At some point, she'd feel the joy she knew it would create. But it was going to take some time. Right now she ached so badly she thought she might die.

* * *

PETE STUMBLED in late and exhausted. Guilt nearly incapacitated him. He'd driven his mother home three hours earlier and then went back to the hospital to sit with his sister just so he could avoid Avery. To be honest, it wasn't Avery he wanted to avoid. It was the conversation they'd have to have. She was hell bent on leaving for France. He was hell bent on staying in Nashville.

His entire life he'd fought to be everything to Avery. How she could just let that go and fly away was beyond him. Sadly he understood it all too well though.

Avery needed something more than to just be a well respected Keller. Moving to France was finding herself.

Perhaps he hadn't been looking at this right at all. If she loved him, as she said she did, she'd realize she couldn't stay away. She'd be running back to him in no time. Surely that would be what would happen. They were meant to be together. It was love—true love.

Pete kicked off his shoes and headed upstairs in the dark and quiet house. He needed to show Avery that he supported her. That would be his secret weapon in getting her back quickly.

He moved into the room and toward the bed. As his eyes adjusted in the dim light of the moon in the window, he could see that she wasn't there.

"Avery?" he called thinking she was in the bathroom, but it too was dark.

Pete stood in the hallway and chills ran over him.

He flicked on the lights and ran back downstairs. The kitchen was bare and there were no signs that she was there or had been.

As he passed back through the living room, he noticed the piece of paper on the coffee table, and he clenched his jaw when he saw the ring.

Did he even need to read the note she'd left? An ache in his chest had him rubbing away the pain with the heel of his hand.

Avery had chosen the unknown over his love.

Pete walked around the couch and sat down. He rested his elbows on his thighs and clasped his hands.

Avery Keller had been his best friend from as far back as he could remember. He'd nursed her broken heart. He'd tucked her in after long nights of celebrating. There hadn't been a family crisis he hadn't seen her through.

Perhaps he'd solely chased her for too long.

Friends helped mold you into the person you became. Avery had certainly helped mold him into the man he'd become.

The ache from his chest moved through him.

A ring left on the table with a note meant it was time to accept that friendships came and went. Even harder was accepting the fact that the love of his life gave up on him.

Pete stood and looked down at the note and the ring.

The pain in his body and his heart was too thick to even consider making it worse by reading the note.

Standing up and walking away, Pete decided he'd look at it

tomorrow when he had to move out of his own house. He guessed he'd better make some phone calls. Not only was his father in the hospital, he was now homeless and jobless. Perhaps it was just a slap to his face to realize the true character of Avery Keller.

Pete swallowed hard. Even though, that's what his mind was thinking, he was sure his heart was going to take a lot longer to truly feel it.

Would there ever be a time when he didn't love Avery?

CHAPTER 18

*I*t was an interesting moment in Avery's life, she decided. There had never been a time when she took a large step in her life and her family hadn't been there.

That was her fault. She'd said her goodbyes to everyone and now she sat in the small municipal airport waiting to board the plane her grandfather had sent for her.

She had never felt so empty and alone.

From the corner of her eye, she saw a man walking right toward her. She closed her eyes and took a breath. In the letter, she'd asked Pete to see her off and to hold her ring until she got back.

This was going to be the hardest goodbye of them all.

When she felt him standing just inches from her, she opened her eyes and looked up.

"I did not mean to interrupt. You look as though you were in prayer," the man said, his French accent thick. "Are you Avery Keller?"

The disappointment, that the man wasn't Pete, dropped into her belly.

"Yes."

He held out his hand. "I am Marcus Bravard. I have come to escort you."

Avery shook his hand. "Nice to meet you."

"If you are ready…"

"Not yet."

Marcus's eyes narrowed quickly then retracted to fit his smile. "Are you waiting for someone? Oh, that is right," he said as if he'd remembered something. "You have someone traveling with us. A Peter Grant."

Avery bit down on her lip. "No. He won't be traveling with us. I would just like to wait a few more minutes. I think he'll be coming to say goodbye."

He nodded. "We must be boarded in twenty minutes."

"I'll be on board," she confirmed.

"Very well." Marcus gave her one last warm smile and walked down the terminal.

She studied him as he walked. He was well over six feet tall and certainly he hadn't flown all the way from Paris in that suit, which wasn't even wrinkled.

He walked very straight and sure of himself, as she assumed a man with great power would. However, if he had any power, why would he be fetching granddaughters for airline flights?

Avery turned her head to look toward the entrance of the airport. If Pete didn't walk through those doors in the next fifteen minutes, she'd never get to say goodbye. She'd never get to confirm that she still loved him.

She waited, wishing he'd run through the door with his suitcase packed, but he never did. After fifteen minutes, she looked toward the jet way and there was Marcus nodding. Time was up. He hadn't come to say goodbye. Asking Pete to stay with her after her birthday had proven to be a big mistake.

* * *

PETE RAN from the parking lot and in through the front door of the airport. Hell, it was small enough he should see her. Still at a sprint he ran down the terminal looking through the windows. There!

He ran toward the door. There was the jet with PIERPONT OIL written on the tail. It was backing away from the gate as he reached for the jet way door.

A woman grabbed him. "Sir, you can't go out there."

"My fiancée! You have to let me out."

The woman's hands gripped his arms tighter. "Sir, the plane is taking off."

Pete stepped back and looked out the window. The jet carrying the woman of his dreams taxied away.

"Can't you stop them? Turn them around," he demanded.

"Your broken heart isn't going to stop that flight," she said with her hands on her hips. "You'd better find a phone and call her in twelve hours."

The woman went back to her work, but kept a steely eye on him as he watched the plane.

It taxied to the end of the runway and a few moments later he watched in disbelief as the plane rose into the air.

She was gone.

* * *

AVERY FELT the push of the jet lift from the ground. She closed her eyes and breathed. What more could she do right now than just breathe?

He hadn't come for her. He didn't say goodbye. It was over.

When the plane leveled off, Marcus stood from his seat and walked to the back of the small plane. He returned a few minutes later with a glass of champagne in a glass flute.

"To celebrate your move to France," he said as he handed her the glass.

"Thank you." She took the glass and sipped it. The bubbles went straight to her head and then landed right in her empty stomach where she quickly pressed her hand. "I should have packed some snacks."

"We have some in the galley. I will get you something."

He rose again and disappeared to the back of the plane. When he returned, he didn't have a bag of chips or a very desired bag of M&M's. Instead, he had a small cheese tray with crackers.

Avery laughed. "That wasn't what I was expecting."

Marcus smiled as he set it on the small table between the seats, which faced each other. He then sat down.

"Your grandfather wants you to be comfortable."

Avery nodded. "I see. How do you know my grandfather?"

Marcus sat back in his seat and crossed his legs. His shoes had a glossy shine to them. This certainly wasn't just some assistant, she thought.

"Your grandfather and I are business acquaintances. I am a wine broker for Pierpont Vineyards, among other things."

"And you happened to be in Nashville on business?"

He smiled as he lifted his glass to his lips. "Napa," he said before sipping. "I promised to escort you home."

Home? She'd just left home. Now she was traveling to somewhere as unfamiliar to her as the wine she'd be making. Actually, she had no idea what part of the wine making process she'd be part of. Truly she'd made a decision on the adventure and not on anything else. Maybe Pete was right. She was selfish. She'd grown up in the shadow of being Simone Pierpont's daughter. Now she just wanted a taste of the lifestyle, but at what cost?

It had already cost her Pete.

She sipped her champagne. To be fair, she'd made this decision before the night of her birthday. She'd been very straightforward with him on her plans to leave. Just because he decided to propose didn't mean she had to feel guilty about trying something new.

Wasn't she already on a private jet having cheese and champagne with a very attractive man? Wasn't she flying to Paris where no doubt a private car would drive her to the vineyard where she would live?

Marcus seemed to understand her position, she thought as she raised her chin a little higher. Her last name might be Keller, but she was Pierpont too. The spitting image of her mother, she could pull off fashion and debutante.

This was her time to build a collection of stories of a jet set life. Hadn't her own parents' story started with a quick affair where her mother abandoned her father on a yacht? A yacht!

She wanted it. She could taste it.

No more rented houses where everyone had lived. No more hand-me-down luxury cars.

Avery Keller was going to be someone she couldn't have been in Nashville.

Finishing the champagne in her flute she looked up at the very handsome Marcus seated across from her. Perhaps the bubbles in her head enhanced his smile, but that was okay. The new Avery Keller didn't have to care.

"Would you mind," she smiled back at him. "I'd love another glass."

Marcus nodded as he reached for her glass. His finger tips brushed her fingers as he took it.

"I will be right back." He stood and walked to the back of the plane.

Avery rested her head against the back of the seat. This was going to be a good life.

CHAPTER 19

*P*ete carried another box into the house where Avery had vacated. Thank God he'd called off the shipping company.

Wasn't it funny that when Avery said she was going to move to France, he said he could move into her place—and here he was.

The house was as familiar to him as any he'd ever lived in. Nearly every Keller he'd known had lived there. He remembered visiting years before when Clara and Christian had lived there. Then Darcy lived in the basement and most recently Julie. Hadn't Avery even told him when she went away that if he moved in maybe the love of his life would move into the basement? It worked out for Ed and Spencer.

He dropped the box in his hands and let it crash to the floor.

His mood was spoiled. He didn't want to think of someone moving into the basement to steal his heart. All he wanted was Avery to turn back around and stop being so stupid. Friend or not, he still cared about her and it didn't look like she'd ever be his wife. But he didn't want to be away from her either.

Pete looked up when he heard the shuffling of feet on the steps. Spencer staggered through the door with a box in his arms.

"Where?"

"Over there," Pete pointed to an empty space where Spencer set down the box.

"How many times am I going to move boxes in and out of this house?" He complained as he straightened his back with his hands on his hips.

"I really appreciate it."

Spencer shrugged. "Man, I'd always help you."

It was a sympathetic copout, Pete thought. But he appreciated his help all the same.

"What are you and Julie doing tonight?"

"Tiffany planned some girls' night out." Spencer rolled his shoulders. "Funny how I get engaged and now my best friend and my fiancée hang out and I get suckered in to moving people."

"Sucks to be you."

"Tell me about it." Spencer laughed. "Want to go get some wings and beer after this? I think there's a game tonight. We could watch at the bar."

That was pretty general, but he knew his friend was trying to help him out, and not just by moving his stuff. He'd spent nearly as much time with Spencer over the years as he had with Avery. They were always together. It didn't surprise him that Spencer would be the one to try and mend Pete's broken heart. Some of that was out of friendship, and some of it was out of guilt since it was his cousin who had broken Pete's heart.

Either way, he'd take the condolences. He might have lost Avery, but he still had Spencer.

Spencer stretched his arms over his head. "I can be thankful you don't own a lot of crap."

Pete laughed. "My mother would argue that it's all still stored in the rafters of the garage."

Spencer nodded. "I've heard that from my mother too. I think we're just good sons. If we took everything away, they'd think we left them for good."

"Right," he said letting the stress release from his shoulders. Spencer was exactly what he'd needed tonight. However, there was one thing weighing very heavy on his mind. "Have you heard from Avery?"

Spencer's eyes flashed and that had given him his answer.

"She called yesterday to say she'd arrived. Simone said she talked to her for a few minutes, but that was all she'd said."

Pete nodded. "I'm glad she arrived safely."

"I can't believe she took off like this. What the hell is wrong with her?"

"She's looking for herself," Pete said.

Spencer shook his head. "She's an idiot. I can say that. She's an idiot." He shoved his hands into the pockets of his jeans. "She had everything with you. I don't understand what she's chasing."

"The life her mother had."

Pete walked toward the kitchen. At least Spencer had brought beer to christen the fridge. He opened the door and pulled out two. Handing one to Spencer, he gave the door a bump with his hip to shut it.

Each of them opened their bottles and took long, deserved swigs.

"I hope she'll be happy," Pete said letting the words sting as he said them.

"I can't believe she didn't call you first."

"She might have. I turned off my phone for a few days. I just couldn't handle it." He pulled out a kitchen chair and sat down. "I'm not stupid enough to think it'll work again. An entire lifetime of friendship and infatuation wasted."

Spencer pulled out a chair, spun it around backward, and sat down with his arms resting on the back.

"Don't think like that. You don't know what she's thinking."

"Yes I do. I've heard every story about Simone Pierpont's life before Nashville. Avery's got the bug. She wants jets and yachts. She wants the life her mother had."

"It's not for real."

"To her it is." Pete took another pull from his bottle. "She left the ring, Spencer. The note said 'see me off' and I missed her. It's over."

He was sure he heard an oath murmured under Spencer's breath as he took a sip of his beer.

In time, he was sure he'd see her again. Their paths were sure to cross at some point. But for now Pete was going to go on. He had an appointment with his investment firm in the morning to grovel for his job back—without promotion.

CHAPTER 20

*H*ills rolled in a green carpet of vines and trees. Avery sat on the small patio out back of her cottage, which sat in the middle of the vineyard.

The coffee in her mug had been sent by her mother in a care package, the beans had anyway. She simply couldn't get that same flavor in France.

She'd lived on the property for nearly a month now, watching the grapes grow on the miles and miles of vines. Her palate for wine had grown and she'd learned quite a bit about the sight, aroma, balances, and harmonies.

Every day she'd walk the rows of vines, as much for quality control as for her sanity. The workers were gracious to her and answered all of her questions. However, she felt as perhaps her grandfather had forgotten her in the little cottage in the vineyard.

He'd never been out to see her, but he was a busy man. The vineyard was not as important to him as his oil business. She understood that. Though she still wasn't sure of her role there.

He'd been very curt to her the day she arrived in France. He'd met her at the airport, and he'd shaken Marcus's hand, but never had he hugged her or touched her.

"Marcus will see to you," he'd said before he'd driven away.

Marcus had been with her nearly every day since.

He'd been instrumental in educating her on the grapes, the vines, and the process. They'd dined together in the small town just beyond the vineyard, and he'd introduced her to employees of the winery and a few local shop owners.

He was kind, and his looks hadn't slipped past her radar. Dark wavy hair and those chocolate eyes had filtered into her dreams a night or two.

He wasn't like the men back home. He was sophisticated and full of knowledge. There was a arrogant side to him, she assumed, that was what made him very successful. Not one moment of the day was wasted, and no one questioned his authority.

She didn't want to say people feared him, but perhaps they did, and that's why they were so attentive to him.

However, that probably came with power in a company. To her he'd been kind.

Avery pulled her sweater closed tighter as a small breeze blew through the vines. It certainly was a different climate than she was used to, though she didn't mind it. The mornings and evenings were much cooler, and during the day the temperature was mild. All things considered, it was perfect.

Today she'd take a walk through the vineyard and then head into town for a few supplies. Marcus was going to pick her up around three and take her to see the fermentation and aging facility. She'd seen the grape pressing the week before.

She had seriously thought she'd be deep into the process by now. Perhaps she'd have an office, a desk, a job title? Avery let out a breath.

At her disposal, she had a Mercedes and an expense account. Her grandfather had an apartment in Paris where she could go and stay anytime. She'd met her grandmother for lunch one day, but that was nearly as foreign to her as the menu, and it made her miss her Grandma Emily something awful.

They certainly were two different kinds of women. Emily was old, very old—but so wise and kind. Her mother's mother was polite and gracious, but not focused on Avery at all. It was all a formality to meet her.

She'd expected that. Her mother hadn't ever talked of her too much, and Avery had only met her a few times. She'd grown up hoping her grandmother would have thought she was special— just as her Grandma Emily had.

Her grandfather, on the other hand, was very attentive—when she'd been in his presence.

He gave her anything she'd needed or wanted—after all, wasn't that why she was there? She wanted to have the car to drive to Paris and stay in a fully furnished apartment overlooking the Eiffel Tower. She wanted to gaze upon the Mona Lisa whenever she felt the urge to walk through the Louvre. Certainly her wardrobe should have been updated with the number of stores her grandfather had arranged credit in.

But it just wasn't right. A piece of her was missing—Pete.

He hadn't called, and she hadn't called him. It was very obvious to her that when he didn't come to the airport that they were over. She missed her friend though.

She'd stalked him on Facebook, but he hadn't posted a thing since she'd left.

When she'd talked to her mother last, she'd learned that Pete's father had heart surgery and was doing very well. Avery had sent him a card and she'd hoped it would prompt Pete to call, but it hadn't.

How could she blame him? Avery had left him for this dream —which wasn't turning out to be very dreamy at all.

The sound of a car driving toward the cottage had her lifting her head and forgetting her woes. She stood from the chair and walked around the small little house to see Marcus pulling up.

He turned off the car and stepped out. He was freshly shaven and perhaps his hair was still damp from his shower.

"Good morning!" He said very enthusiastically and then stopped and looked her over. "You are not ready."

"Ready for what?"

"Our tour."

Avery stared at him and then looked down at her bulky sweater and lounge pants. "I thought you said around three."

He smiled and moved toward her. His dark eyes sparkled as he looked down at her. "I added some adventure to our day." Marcus placed his hands on her arms and stood gazing at her.

Avery's body quaked at the intimacy of his touch. He'd never touched her before quite like this.

She swallowed hard. "What did you have planned?"

"Your grandfather has given us his yacht for the weekend. Pack a bag and a swimming suit."

Avery gripped her coffee mug between her hands. "Marcus, I don't…"

"I have invited friends," he said. His accent was thick and romantic.

He moved in closer and she could smell the fresh soap and cologne on him. Her body seemed to stir in his presence.

"You cannot stay here in your little cottage forever. You must enjoy too." He lifted his hand to her cheek and her breath caught in her lungs. "What is keeping you from enjoying your time here?"

Did he really want an answer to that? "I'm just not sure what my grandfather had planned for me."

Marcus smiled and it lit into his eyes. "He wants you to be happy. He can offer that." His thumb brushed her cheekbone. "I can help him offer that."

The air that her lungs had held hostage sucked into her

stomach and landed as a heavy weight. He was gazing at her, nearly holding her. She'd had enough men make a move on her to know that was what was going on, but why?

"Marcus, I..."

He pressed his index finger to her lips. "Go pack and get ready. I have croissants in the car. I will fix you a plate for breakfast."

Tucking a wisp of her fallen hair behind her ear, he gave her a wink. Things had changed in the past few days. She thought she was just becoming comfortable, but he seemed to think there was more.

CHAPTER 21

*A*very went inside and up to her bedroom. She gathered a few clothing items and her swimsuit. Why she was doing this was beyond her. She wanted to do real work. When was her grandfather going to put her in charge of something? When did the work begin that she'd been looking forward to—whatever it was.

Avery started the shower and ran a brush through her hair as she waited for the water to get warm.

She thought about a weekend out on her grandfather's yacht, and she wondered if it were the same one her mother had abandoned her father on.

Perhaps a few days away to enjoy the life she'd come for was just as in order as waiting her grandfather out. Yes, she'd go, meet new people, and work on her tan. She'd send pictures to her mother. Instead of having this void between them, perhaps they could bond over like experiences.

Marcus had mentioned that he'd invited friends. That would be good. She needed to meet more people and she certainly didn't want to be alone with Marcus. They didn't know each other quite that well.

She brushed her hair back.

They had spent a lot of time together the past month, she thought. Wasn't that how people got to know each other?

He was kind and warm to her, but she'd seen his frightening anger fly a few times. However, it wasn't aimed at her, but usually at a worker who hadn't done their job. As she didn't know her own job, she couldn't tell when someone wasn't doing theirs.

People seemed to do what Marcus wanted them to do. She wondered what it was like to have that kind of power. Would that come in time? Was she strong enough to use that kind of power?

A PLATE with croissants and fruit was on the table with a cup of tea and a folded napkin. Marcus's voice came from the other room. He was on a phone call, she assumed, as she could only hear one side of the conversation.

Avery sat down and began to eat the food he'd set out for her.

"I see you packed."

She looked up to see him standing in the doorway. "Yes."

"Good. I thought maybe you would try to change your mind. I am glad you did not."

She wasn't sure what to say. In the back of her mind, she still felt the twinge that something wasn't right about it. However, she'd left Nashville to live this life and if she didn't start living it then the trip was a waste—and she'd given up too much not to enjoy every moment of it.

He set her cell phone on the table in front of her. "Your phone rang while you were in the shower. I answered it."

Avery slid the phone closer to her. "Who was it?"

"I believe it was the man you had wanted to accompany you on your trip."

"Pete?" His name croaked out and panicked zipped through her.

Marcus smiled. "I think he did say that was his name."

Avery began scrolling through the phone looking for a text message or something. Had something gone wrong? His father? His family? Him? "What did he say?"

"I told him you were packing for a cruise on the yacht and when we returned you would phone him."

Her muscles tightened. "That's how you said it?" She scrolled through the contacts to his number. "I have to call him now."

Marcus rested a hand atop of hers, stopping her process. "The call can wait. We are leaving now."

PETE SAT ON HIS COUCH, now misplaced in Avery's living room. His phone was cupped in his hands and his broken heart was shattered into even smaller pieces.

What had he expected? Avery had chosen the life she'd dreamed about over everything else. It should be no surprise that he was part of the everything else.

It had been a month and was she even aware of the month he'd had?

He'd groveled to get his job back, but it didn't come with the promotion. His father had surgery. Wasn't that a taxing time? More than anything he'd wished she'd have been there to comfort him. How many times had he sat in waiting rooms of hospitals for her?

Pete shook his head. Setting his phone on the coffee table, he leaned back on the couch and rubbed his eyes. It was past two o'clock in the morning and it had been another long day.

Today hadn't been about him or his father. Today's drama belonged to his mother. Hearing her mutter the words, "I have cancer," kicked him in the balls.

A month ago Avery would have been there hearing her say the

words, holding his hand. Since that wasn't an option, he'd called Avery's cousin Christian.

Christian was a good shoulder to cry on. His own mother battled cancer when Christian was young. He knew what Pete was going through.

He'd met him at the bar Christian's brother-in-law, Warner Wright, owned downtown. It had been crowded, but that worked out just fine for Pete.

OF COURSE, when you cried on one Keller shoulder, you cried on them all. He'd called Christian, but by the end of the night Christian's older brother Ed, their sister Clara, and their cousins Spencer and Tyler were all at the table comforting him. The only person missing was Avery.

They couldn't assure him it would all be all right. What they could ensure was they would be right there with him the entire time. Avery might be out of the picture, but he still belonged with them all.

Pete's mind went back to the man's voice on the phone. A thick French accent and an in-charge tone when he spoke. He couldn't help but wonder who he was.

Honestly, he shouldn't care. Avery hadn't held up her end of the relationship. It would only figure she'd moved on.

She'd wanted to feel out those Pierpont roots. He supposed she had now.

Pete picked up his cell phone and hit the power button on the side. He was too tired to even climb the stairs to bed.

He set the phone back down and pulled the afghan his mother had crocheted off the back of the couch. Wrapping himself in the comfort of its stitches, he lie down on the couch and let the day take him under.

CHAPTER 22

They were getting married. Pete couldn't be happier as he watched his bride walking toward him. The veil covered her face, but he knew who it was.

Family surrounded them. Birds chirped in nearby trees, and his best man gave him a solid slap on the back.

Pete looked up at him, but who was he? Certainly if he were marrying Avery he'd have chosen Spencer to stand with him.

"Who are you?"

The man smiled and said, "I think you are in my space."

His accent was deep and heavy. French.

This wasn't his wedding. Avery wasn't walking toward him though he still couldn't see her face.

Suddenly an enormous crash pierced his ears and Pete sat up in a cold sweat. He was on his couch, in the living room, and it was daylight.

The man was gone. The bride to be was gone. He was alone.

"Shit!"

He heard the word yelled from the backyard and it took him a moment to realize someone was outside.

Pete scrambled to his feet and ran to the backdoor.

In the driveway, he could see a big, old, blue Ford pickup truck full of boxes. Knelt down beside the truck was a woman with a blonde ponytail high on the top of her head bent over a box of broken plates.

"Can I help you?" Pete called from the back porch, his eyes batting to focus in the sun.

"Sorry. I dropped this box and of course it had all my dishes. They're just Walmart dishes, but I think I might have broken every single one of them. This is the worst." She rolled her head from side to side. "Well, in hindsight it isn't really bad at all. It's just some cheap plates. I can eat off of something else for a few days until I can buy a new plate. Start small, you know. One at a time."

Pete batted his eyes again, but this time to try and clear the cobwebs out of his head.

The woman finished loading the few shards that had escaped back into the box, then stood and stretched her back.

"This is a lovely morning, isn't it? It's days like this I wish I were a runner." Then she laughed and looked down at herself. "Right, as if I'd ever run."

He gave her a look. She was soft—yeah, soft. But he was sure she was criticizing her body. Women, his sisters mostly, did that all the time.

"Anyway," she stopped, pushed the sunglasses from her eyes and rested them atop her head. She looked him over and smiled. "You must think I'm a nit. Here I am screaming obscenities early on a Saturday morning, and you obviously were sleeping. Trust me, I'll be a very quiet neighbor. This really isn't like me at all. I don't usually…" She stopped, took a breath, and started toward him.

Pete blinked again against the sun as the woman walked up the steps of the porch.

She reached out her hand. "I'm Jill. Jill Yance. I'm going to be living downstairs."

Pete nodded as she shook his hand and then realized the entire time he hadn't had a chance to say anything.

"Pete."

"Nice to meet you, Pete." She smiled a smile that was nearly as bubbly as her personality and Pete realized he might have smiled back. "I'll let you get back to sleep and I'll try to be quiet."

Pete nodded as she pulled her hand back and started down the steps.

"Hey, Jill." He heard his own voice call out to her. "Let me brush my teeth and I'll come help. Those stairs are steep."

"Awesome!" she shouted back to him as she pulled the sunglasses back down over her eyes—which were a baby blue.

He'd noticed her eyes.

He'd noticed her.

Okay, he thought as he headed back into the house, he wasn't dead from a broken heart.

PETE RETURNED FIFTEEN MINUTES LATER. He had two cups of coffee, one in each hand, and a plate tucked under his arm.

"I thought you could use some coffee and I had an extra plate," he said as he walked up to the back of the pickup truck where Jill was moving boxes.

"How attached are you to that plate? You see I'm not any kind of good luck charm."

Pete laughed. He actually laughed for the first time in a month. "No sentimental value attached."

Jill rested her fists on her hips and looked at him. "Are you attached to the mug?" She nodded to another box of broken items. "I could use one of those as well.

Now the laughter rolled from him. Was there some kind of God that knew he needed a breath of fresh air? Jill seemed to be that today.

"Cup is all yours," he said lifting it in the air so she could reach it. "I didn't flavor it or anything, but I have some cream in the house if you want some."

She looked down into the mug. "You wouldn't be offended?"

"No. You wouldn't be the only woman who took my coffee and made it taste good."

"Good, because this looks very dark." She handed him back the mug and jumped out of the back of the truck bed before taking it back. She took the plate from him and stowed it in another box. When she looked back at him, she gave him a satisfied nod. "Thanks for the plate. Now show me the way to the creamer."

He couldn't help but take a moment to stare at the woman he'd just met. She was so different from anyone he'd ever known. Her energy was contagious and he found himself smiling at her—which she noticed.

"What's wrong?"

"Nothing at all."

She slowly nodded. "You're smiling really weird. Listen, if you're some kind of creeper, I'll tell that John guy I don't want to rent this place."

He raised an eyebrow. "Even if I tell you I'm not some creeper wouldn't that be hard to believe? I mean a creeper would be hell bent on making sure you didn't think he was one. What if you're the creeper?"

Jill rested a hand on his shoulder as she laughed at him. "I'm going to take my chances. Now get me to that creamer before this coffee is cold."

Pete led her up the back steps and into the house.

Jill stopped as she entered. "This is nice."

"Thanks. The last tenant left the lacey curtains. I didn't choose those."

"Not judging," she said. "So you know John too? The guy who rented me the basement?"

"I've known John most of my life. I'm a family friend," he

added, but he felt as though he should have just said he was part of the family.

"That's cool. You could fill me in then."

Pete opened the refrigerator and took out the creamer and handed it to her.

"Thanks. Do you have a spoon too?"

He opened a drawer and took out a spoon.

"How long have you lived here?" she asked as she perfected the coffee and then took the spoon to stir it.

"About a month."

"John told me the tenant from my apartment moved out and is getting married. What about this tenant?"

Pete swallowed the hard knot that had lodged in his throat. "She moved to France."

"No way!" She looked up at him. "Moved to France? That's about the coolest thing I've ever heard."

He wished he could be as excited about it, but that just wasn't the case.

Jill sipped her coffee, added more cream, and sipped again. "Now that's the perfect cup of coffee."

Pete wasn't so sure. He liked it just the way he'd brewed it.

Jill set the spoon in the sink and replaced the creamer before resting up against the counter. "Why did she move to France?"

Pete shrugged. "Opportunity. Family. Her mother is from there, and she wanted to know a different life," he bit out the words.

A smile formed on Jill's mouth from behind her cup. "There's a story there."

He drank down his coffee, which was growing cold. "Not anymore there isn't."

"I get it. You don't know me. I don't know you. Why share your secrets with the woman standing in your kitchen having coffee, who will hear every time you flush the toilet."

He laughed immediately. She sure had a way of making him feel at ease.

"She was my best friend growing up. We finally committed to seeing each other, and got engaged."

Her eyes opened wide. "She left you for France," she simply stated, and he saluted with his mug in response. "Oh, Pete, I'm sorry."

"Me too."

"You're still together?"

He gave it a moment of thought and then shook his head. "I don't think the forever was meant to be. I dearly miss my friend though."

Jill drank down her coffee—or mug of cream, he considered. She then rinsed it out and placed it in the sink.

"It's a good thing I'm moving in. I'm a great friend. Not huge into the dating thing. Not gay," she added. "My mom keeps asking since she thinks I should be dating—men. Then she follows it up with, you have a pretty face, as if that will rid twenty pounds off of me."

"For the record you do have a pretty face, and an infectious personality."

She studied him. "Infectious as in you're sick now?"

"As in I could do with a little more of you. I haven't laughed in a month. I've known you twenty minutes, and I've laughed a few times now."

"Then that's good, right?"

"Very."

"Thanks for thinking my face is pretty."

He could feel the heat rise in his cheeks. "I noticed your eyes right away too. I don't see a thing wrong with you, but I have sisters. Girls always think there is something wrong with them."

"My jean size."

"See what I mean? I happen to think your jeans look exceptionally nice on you."

Jill narrowed her eyes on him. "You're not a creeper?"

"Not even close."

"Genuine through and through?"

"To a fault."

She nodded. "Are you still going to help me move?"

He laughed again and it was freeing. "I am also a man of my word."

"Hmmm." She pushed back from the counter. "I think I could fall in love with you. I won't," she assured him. "I'll think about it, but you're still in love with the French girl. But we can see what time brings."

She gave him a wink, opened the back door, and walked out of the kitchen.

There was a little wiggle in her step and he wondered if he'd given her the pick-me-up she'd needed because she'd sure given him one.

CHAPTER 23

*C*hampagne was chilling in a silver bucket. The bubbles from the crystal flute she held to her lips tickled her nose.

Sea air blew through her hair, and the late afternoon sun on her skin warmed her.

Laughter from people on the deck filled her ears. The thought that her mother had taken a yacht out into the French Rivera, or the Côte d'Azur, as she'd been corrected, humored her. It was unbelievable to her that her mother could drive a yacht, or a boat of any kind, and that she'd left Avery's father there to get home on his own.

Knowing the love they had, her mother must have seriously doubted what was to be.

Was she afraid of losing everything? Did she second-guess their affair?

Avery sipped from her glass. Her mother had been very open about that time. She'd wanted the affair to be true love, but she was sure it was only sex. Though, she was sure it was sex for her, and a relationship for him.

Avery wasn't sure, sometimes, if it was good to know all her parents' secrets. Perhaps that came with being an only child.

She let the sun soak her face with warmth as she thought about her mother living like this every day—shopping, lunching, yachting, and spa-ing. Hadn't Avery dreamed of this her whole life? Her grandfather was making it a reality. She hadn't done much but toured facilities since she'd been there. There had been no work done on her part to earn what she was given. Was it possible it would all be too much in the end?

"Perhaps more sunscreen for you," Marcus sat down in the lounge adjacent to hers, his body turned to sit facing her.

"Am I burning up?"

He opened the bottle in his hand and squirted the white lotion into the palm of his hand.

"Come. Sit up now," he instructed.

Avery did as he said, turning her back to him. She felt his hands press to her skin and she held her breath.

She missed the touch of a man. Something like this was very intimate, she thought as he slid his hands over her shoulders and down her arms.

"Your skin is very hot. Perhaps we should go in and lie down."

Avery realized her mouth had gone dry as Marcus moved to her lounge and sat next to her.

He trailed a finger down her arm. "I can make you a nice drink inside."

She sucked in a breath as Marcus reached his hand to her cheek.

"I make you uncomfortable."

"I wasn't expecting this."

Marcus smiled. He lifted his glasses to the top of his head and let his deep, dark eyes lock onto hers.

"Why not? We have been attracted to each other since I accompanied you from Nashville."

"Is that so?"

"Do not play games with me, Avery. I know you have thought about this." He moved in closer to her and pressed his lips to hers firmly.

Every muscle in Avery's body began to shake. This wasn't what she wanted, was it?

The captain came on the deck walking toward Marcus.

"Sir, Mr. Pierpont is calling."

Marcus looked up at the captain. "For me?"

"Yes, Sir."

Marcus dismissed him with a nod and looked back at Avery. "I will be just a moment. Do not move."

She watched him pass by her and head inside. Her heart still hammered in her chest.

Avery looked around and realized that there was no one even near enough to hear her if something went wrong out on that boat. The only people there were the friends of Marcus' that he'd brought along. Why was she worried anything would happen? She pressed her hands to her thighs and took in a deep breath.

Where did he get the impression they were romantically involved or that she was interested? Would he have kissed her if he'd thought otherwise?

She pulled her phone from the small bag next to her lounge and walked toward the railing of the boat. Since that morning, when Marcus had told her Pete called, she'd wanted to return his call, but Marcus had hovered over her. She hadn't really noticed, until then, that he'd been doing that for the better part of a month.

Wherever she wanted to go, he was sure to be there or arrange the travel. He decided the restaurants they would eat at and the facilities they would tour. She'd seen many wonderful works of art, but he'd chosen those too.

It was as if she weren't allowed to make the decisions for them. Marcus was in control of everything, including who she called and when.

Avery scrolled through her contacts. Why had Pete called? Did he want to apologize for not coming to the airport? Did he miss her? A nervous flutter filled her stomach. Certainly if something happened to his father someone would have called, not just Pete.

Oh, who cared why he called. Right now she needed him. She needed the comfort of her friend. Nothing was going as planned.

She looked at the screen in the early afternoon sun. It was hard to tell if it was even on.

Avery cupped her hand over it to see. Who had she been kidding? Did she think she'd actually have cell service in the middle of the water?

She'd just go back inside and place the call.

This was bigger than she was now. She needed off the boat. Marcus kissing her had thrown her for a loop. Avery had come to prove to herself and her grandfather that she could be someone. She hadn't expected Marcus's advances.

Hands came down on her shoulders startling her and she lost her hold on her phone. It tumbled from her hands and out into the water.

"My phone! Oh, no!"

CHAPTER 24

$\mathcal{A}$very looked down into the water, but there was no sign of her phone anywhere.

Marcus laughed as he pressed his body to her back, his hands still firm on her shoulders.

"We will buy you a new one when we return. For now you do not need it."

Avery spun around to confront him only to find herself pressed against him, the railing pushing into her back.

"You are exquisite, Avery." He brushed his fingers through her hair. "You are like a painting that should hang in a gallery for all people to admire."

She felt her jaw drop and the air in her lungs expel on a gasp.

Marcus gave her that smile that twisted her insides. "Your grandfather is on his way."

"Here?"

"Yes. He would like to spend some time with his grand-daughter."

Avery bit down on her bottom lip. "Wonderful. I thought he'd forgotten about me."

"He has plans for you." He moved in and again pressed a kiss to her lips. "We have plans."

Those words didn't sit well with her at all.

Marcus stepped back. "You should go inside and take a shower. Make yourself presentable for when your grandfather arrives. I will have the chef begin supper."

Avery nodded. It took an entire staff to run the boat on which she was just lounging.

She walked around Marcus, picked up her bag, and headed toward her room all the while he watched her as if he were making sure she wouldn't leave the boat.

Perhaps the life of an oil heiress, or vineyard heiress, wasn't what it was cracked up to be. People served her without expecting respect or thank you. She was "handled" all the time. Free to do whatever her grandfather or Marcus permitted, but not to find her own way or do what she wanted.

There hadn't been time for her to make her own life there.

She was missing barbecue from Steve's Barbecue Pit and Beer, homemade strudel from her grandmother, and her mother's horrible meatloaf.

This had been the longest she'd been away from home, and it was starting to weigh heavyily on her.

She'd missed four Sundays of dinners.

The babies born the day after her birthday were already a month old. She should call Courtney and see how she was feeling, she thought, and then remembered the fate of her phone.

Avery walked through the door of her room and quickly turned and locked it behind her. The last thing she needed was Marcus walking in while she was in the shower giving her demands as to how to dress for her own grandfather's visit. Right now that would be something she just couldn't handle.

She started the water in the shower, undressed, and stepped in. The smell of the suntan lotion filled her nose as it washed off her skin along with the memory of Marcus's touch.

Tears began to sting her eyes. What was she doing here? Why had this been so important?

Avery washed the lazy day off her skin and let the water soothe her. It was then she heard the sound of a helicopter and the boat shifted a bit.

She braced herself as she stepped out of the shower as much for the shift of the boat as the shift in her heart. It was time to tell her grandfather she'd made a mistake and would like to go home.

Certainly he would understand. After all, it didn't seem as though he wanted her there anyway. Her being there didn't seem as important to him as it had a few months ago when she'd visited him.

AVERY WALKED out to the deck. She wore a long sundress that blew in the warm breeze. She'd piled her hair in a loose bun atop her head and the air on her neck gave her a chill.

"You look beautiful," Marcus said from behind her.

She turned to see him, dressed as if he were going to a formal dinner and not one on a boat.

"Your grandfather is resting and will be up in just a bit."

Avery nodded nervously.

"It looks as though we will have a beautiful sunset this evening."

He moved toward her and she pushed her shoulders back, inching her chin in the air.

"How long is my grandfather staying?"

"For the evening. He is a very busy man."

"He is."

Marcus was now in front of her reaching for her wrists. "He is very happy that you are enjoying yourself." He brushed his fingers up her arms. "You are enjoying yourself, are you not?"

Avery swallowed hard. "I am enjoying myself. But I have to admit, I'm confused by your reaction to me today."

Marcus raised his hand to her neck and cupped it. "I am a man who get's what he wants. I want you."

"Me? Why?"

"*Ma chérie,* you have become my obsession." His eyes narrowed as he spoke.

"Marcus, I…"

He pressed a finger to her lips. "You are here in France. Romanic, beautiful, France. Enjoy what it offers—romance." He took the finger from her lips and held it up as if to keep her attention.

Marcus reached into his pocket and took out a black felt box. When he opened it there was a beautiful opal necklace winking up at her in the oncoming sunset.

"Oh, Marcus…"

"Turn. Let me put this on you."

Something told her she shouldn't accept it, but how could she help herself?

She turned and felt him against her as he draped the chain around her neck and then pressed a kiss to her skin.

Her knees went weak and her eyes closed as Marcus's hands slid down her arms.

"You are shaking," he whispered in her ear.

"I'm very nervous."

Marcus turned her to face him. "I want my touch to only make you quiver because I excite you, not because you are nervous." He cupped her face in his hands. "I will show you what we could have."

He lowered his head and moved his mouth against hers. Avery's eyes closed again, and she was taken under by his touch and his warm, possessive kiss.

CHAPTER 25

The weekend on the yacht had become so much more, Avery realized as she sat in the back of a car being driven through the streets of Paris toward her grandfather's apartment, which he kept there.

Her grandfather had pleasantly surprised her by telling her that she'd be meeting with investors in Paris, which she'd just done.

He'd given her a plan of action to make the wine label take flight. Everything for the meeting had been nearly scripted for her, but she'd been more than prepared.

This was why she was in France, and now she felt the empowerment she'd been looking for. Was this how her mother felt when she'd walked into meetings concerning her grandfather's oil business? Avery remembered her mother saying that she attended most of the meetings concerning the building of her father's buildings, which he usually contracted with Avery's uncle Zach.

Avery touched the necklace that brushed her neck and her mouth went dry. She'd spent a week on that yacht, not only a weekend as Marcus had first intended. Her grandfather had flown in and gone just as quickly. Marcus' friends had then gone back, and soon it was only her and Marcus on the yacht with the staff catering to their every need.

Heat rose in her cheeks, and she used her breath to calm herself.

Marcus had seduced her, and she'd fallen for his words, his kisses, touches, and his promises—pliant from much too much wine. There had been some fear, but she assumed that had been her own demon. Marcus wasn't Pete.

She held her hand out in front of her and clenched it when it shook.

The thoughts going through her head only damned her. She hadn't meant to move on without Pete—not really. And it was fuzzy to her when had the exact moment been she'd given up that control. She straightened in the seat and gripped her clutch tightly in her lap.

She wanted to embrace her Pierpont side, well now she had. Until the right man came along, what did it matter what she did? What if Marcus was that man? After all, he came to the airport to fetch her when Pete didn't even have the nerve to show up.

She gripped her clutch even tighter. No, she wasn't going to go down that road in her mind. Marcus had made it very clear to her that they were now exclusive, and she was his.

Clenching her teeth, she thought about the moment when he'd made that perfectly clear to her.

Part of her wished she'd spoken up and told him that wasn't how she thought a man treated a woman, but what position was she in to do that? She was at the mercy of Marcus and her grandfather.

Her grandfather's trust in the man somehow had gotten her exactly what she'd wanted—a position of power. She supposed she had used Marcus as much as perhaps he'd used her.

Well, she was in it for the ride and now there was no turning back. The Avery Keller that had left Nashville wasn't the same one who had just wooed a team of investors to buy into the vineyard.

Avery pulled the new phone Marcus had purchased for her out of her clutch and looked it over. The only person, other than Marcus, that she had called on it was her mother.

It had taken nearly a bottle of wine to keep her voice steady when she'd spoken to her too. But Avery was very convincing that she was doing fine and she hoped her mother was fooled by her words.

There was, however, one thing that kept coming to mind as she looked at her phone, the contacts now missing and empty, what had Pete wanted that morning?

She should call him. It had been nearly a month and a half since she'd spoken to him. They could be civil. She could still be his friend. It would be a waste of twenty years if they couldn't even be friends.

Her life had moved on from Nashville. She was, after all, a powerful woman now. Certainly she could talk to her best friend and convey that things were fine with her and she hoped he was doing well too.

She looked at the watch Marcus had bought her at the Rolex store before he headed back to the vineyard for a meeting. It shimmered with its diamonds. It was nearly noon. Back home Pete would just be heading out for work. Maybe if she caught him during his commute he would take the time to talk to her.

Avery closed her eyes and took a deep breath before she dialed his number.

CHAPTER 26

*P*ete took off his shoes and socks, then tiptoed over the wet towels on Jill's bathroom floor. The flood of water coming out from under her sink was making a mess of the place.

He'd called John, but it would still be a half hour before he could get there. They had to do something now.

"Your suit is going to get ruined," Jill said as Pete got down on his knees.

"It'll get wet. I'll change in a moment." He took the wrench with him under the cabinet and began to turn off the water source. He was no plumber that was for sure.

As water sprayed him in he face, he could hear his phone ring in his suit pocket, which he'd hung on the door knob. "Get that, Jill. I'm expecting a call from an investor."

He could hear her laugh as towels sloshed under her feet.

"I got it. I got it. Hello?" He heard her saying over the noise of the water still rushing toward him as he turned the valve. "This is Jill." He heard her walking closer as the water finally subsided. "Yeah, he's here. Can you hold on just a moment, he's getting the water turned off. This morning isn't going quite the way we planned. We're having some plumbing problems."

Pete pulled himself out from under the sink. She might have been right. His suit might have been ruined.

Wasn't Jill a sight in her pajamas and her hair piled atop her head talking away to who ever kept her attention on the other end of his phone?

"He has emerged. Have a great day," she added as she handed him the phone.

Pete covered the phone with his hand. "Go up and use my shower or you're going to be late."

"You're too good to me. Can I use a towel too?" She asked as she started down the hall. "Mine are all under you on the floor."

He laughed as he lowered his hand. "Yes."

When he heard her take the steps that went up to his kitchen inside the house he lifted the phone to his ear.

"Thanks for holding. This is Pete."

"Hi," was all she said and his heart jumped into his throat.

"Avery?"

"Who's Jill?"

That was her first question? It had been nearly two months since he talked to her. Some man answered her phone and told him that when they returned from their vacation she'd call him back. What the hell kind of vacation had she taken? Who the hell was she to ask who Jill was? He should just hang up on her. Goddamn she made him mad.

"She's a good friend," he said hoping to drive a point home. Not that he knew what point that was, but he hoped she felt it. "She lives in the apartment."

"John rented it to her?"

"Yep. Good things come from this basement. It worked for Ed and Spencer. Didn't you tell me that once?"

He heard the air release in her sigh. "I did."

"She's full of spunk too. She makes me laugh a lot," he tried to say lightly, "So how was your vacation?" He felt the bite in his words so he was sure she hadn't missed his tone.

"It was lovely, thank you."

It was lovely. Already she had a snooty tone to her. Maybe fate stepped in that day when he missed her at the airport.

"That's good."

"Marcus said you'd called that morning. I went to call you back, but I dropped my phone overboard."

He clucked his tongue. "Musta been one helluva party."

"Clumsy me really."

"Doesn't actually sound like you at all." His hair dripped down into his eyes and he scooped it back. "So, how's it going? How's the wine business?"

"Fine, thank you. I'm just leaving an investors' meeting in Paris. It looks like we'll be in some very fine restaurants next month."

His defenses with her were breaking down the longer her voice rang in his ear. The pang of her void was now pressing down on his chest

"I'm very proud of you, Avery. We all are."

Did he hear her sniff? Was she crying? "That means a lot to me."

An awkward silence fell between them. That had never happened before.

"It was very nice to hear from you," Pete said wringing his shirttails on the floor. "I'm going to be late for work if I don't get changed. The pipes in Jill's apartment burst under the bathroom sink. I'm soaked in my newest suit. Had to send her upstairs to shower." He hadn't realized just how much Jill had rubbed off on him. He smiled listening to himself ramble.

"Pete, before you go, why did you call that day?"

He felt the blood drain from his head and he backed up to the toilet and sat down on the closed seat.

"I was desperate to talk to you—my friend."

"I'm still your friend, Pete. Nothing has changed there."

Yes, it had, he thought. It all changed.

"Right." He scooped another handful of wet hair back and let out a breath. "Did you know my dad had surgery? Funny you can have heart surgery and be back to your self in a few days."

"My mom told me. I'm glad to hear he's doing well. I sent a card."

He knew that. It was up on the mantel like a trophy. How many times had he looked at it just to see her handwriting?

"The day I called you, I'd spent the day with my mom." He groaned. "And the evening with your cousins drinking it away."

"How is your mother? Is everything okay?"

Pete pressed his lips together. He wasn't going to cry like a baby to Avery, but he could feel the tears burning.

"No. Yesterday she started chemo."

"Chemo?" Her voice rose through the phone. "Pete, she has cancer?"

Even the words hurt. "Yes. They're very optimistic. They caught it early. Ed and Christian walked me through what will happen."

"I'll call her."

That brought a smile to his mouth. "She'd like that. They miss you, Avery." He couldn't help it. It was true.

"I miss everyone too."

Pete looked up and Jill stood in the doorway only wrapped in his towel. He hadn't touched the woman, and Avery wasn't his to have anymore, so why did he feel so guilty looking at Jill's beautiful curves?

"I need my hair pick," she whispered pointing to the cabinet.

Pete nodded and pulled it from the drawer. He handed it to her, and when she smiled, the guilt over looking at her shot straight to his gut.

"Avery, I need to go. Call my mom. She'd love to hear from you. Courtney would like you to call too. She's not having a great time with this pregnancy, and every little thing that can cheer her up helps."

"I'll do that."

"Bye, Avery."

He waited a moment for her to say goodbye, but instead he heard. "I love you."

He'd heard it loud and clear, but he disconnected the call. He didn't need to drag it out any further. There was no need.

"Avery?" Jill asked as she ran the pick through her hair.

"Yup." He looked at the clock on his phone. No matter what, he was going to be late. "I'd better get going."

"Everything okay?" she asked as he stood.

"I think she's lonely."

"Reconsidering her move?"

He shook his head. "I don't think so. Not sure why she called."

Maybe he'd call in sick. Suddenly he wasn't feeling so well.

He pushed back his wet hair one more time as he stood and walked toward the door.

Jill backed up to let him through, but he stopped right in front of her. Her eyes grew wide, and he realized just how close their bodies were.

She was so different with her curves and her softness compared to Avery and her sculpted, toned, yoga body. The desire to touch her was clearing the anger Avery had brought out in him.

It was time. Avery was his past. A great past, but that was over.

He took another step toward Jill. She backed up against the doorjamb and sucked in a breath.

Without a word he raised his hands to her face, cupping her cheeks, and pulled her to him for a long, deep, satisfying kiss.

When he eased back, her eyes were still wide, and he was sure she still hadn't taken a breath.

"Have a good day. Maybe we can catch some dinner," he said as he stepped away.

Jill only nodded and Pete smiled. He'd never kissed anyone into a trance.

Perhaps the day could get better he thought as he walked out of her apartment and up the steps with a little bit of a skip in his step.

a very bit down on her lip as he line went dead on the other end. Had he heard her? Did he know what she'd said to him?

Tears began to fall as the driver pulled up to the apartment building. She wiped them away as quickly as she could. No one could see her like that.

She put on her Chanel sunglasses, which she thought made her look like Audrey Hepburn. Gripping her clutch in her hands, she sucked in that Pierpont aristocrat and that Keller courage. No one would see her crack over a man she loved, and who was obviously preoccupied with Jill.

Jill. The name resonated in her head. *Good things come from the basement. Didn't you tell me that?* She could smack her head against the window for telling him that.

He should have come to France with her, and it would have all been okay.

She clenched her jaw and fought from sinking down into the seat as the driver stopped.

Avery thought that had she just stayed in Nashville with Pete everything would have been okay. They'd have been there for each other while his father had surgery, and now while his mother underwent chemo. It should have been her in the basement helping him clean up the water mess. In the midst of the chaos, they'd be planning their wedding. She and Julie could have been wedding dress shopping together.

She looked down at her hands and thought of the ring that had adorned her finger for such a brief time.

Had even the thought of them been a mistake?

No. She couldn't believe that. Nothing with Pete had ever been a mistake.

The driver opened the door and Avery stepped out of the back as if she'd been doing it her whole life to have such grace. It felt good and that Pierpont power surged through her making her forget the momentary thoughts of what could have been had she stayed.

The man at the door to the building gave her a nod and she returned it with a curt little nod as well.

When she reached her apartment, she slid the key in the door, pushed it open, and then made sure it was locked securely before she literally fell onto the floor and cried.

They were wasted tears. She was lonely, that was all. Perhaps a trip back to Nashville would soothe her. She could regroup, and then focus back on the business that had been so important it had her giving up family just to be there.

Yes, that's what she'd do. When Marcus called, she'd let him know her plans. Her grandfather would probably approve. Wouldn't he understand what she'd left to take him up on his offer?

The tears began to dry and she pulled herself up off the floor and walked to the kitchen to make a pot of tea.

MARCUS WAS furious on the other end of the phone when Avery told him of her plans to go home for a visit.

"You have just met with investors who will need to be taken care of. This idiotic idea that you go back to America is ridiculous. You've only been here over a month. Your grandfather will think it is ridiculous as well."

"Marcus, I would be gone all of a week."

"That is not an option, Avery. I forbid you to go."

She took a breath to argue his forbidding. Who did he think he was commanding her like that?

But his demanding words cut her off. "Now the driver will pick you up precisely at eight in the morning. You have a meeting with a bottle designer. He knows what we want, you are just to admire his work. Do I make myself clear?"

"Perfectly."

"Do not be late. I am not going to discuss this with your grandfather. Again, you have been absurd in your thoughts. I do not recommend you bring it up to him either. I am very disappointed."

Avery clenched her jaw. "Marcus, I'm a grown woman. You can't tell me what to do."

"I can as long as you are being thoughtless. Your life is here with me now. We agree."

"No, you agreed to that."

"Avery, you agreed to that when you accepted my gifts and let me take you to bed. Now you will be mindful."

The vile taste of disrespect for him, and herself, rose in her throat. How could she have been so foolish and careless? How could she have thought that it would make the memory and the feelings for Pete just go away? Was that what she had thought? So much of that week was an absolute blur.

Her mother had admitted to playing these kinds of games in the past with men. How had she survived them? How had her heart made it through them?

"I must go, Avery. You be on time tomorrow. The driver will

bring you back in the afternoon and we will meet with your grandfather for dinner. Goodnight."

The line disconnected and she sat on the loveseat and stared down at the phone. He had no right to talk to her like that. Tomorrow she would tell him exactly what she thought of his behavior. She may have, in a weak and horrible moment, given her body to him, but not claim. She may have accepted his many gifts, but just as easily she could give them back.

She was Avery Keller and no one pushed her around.

CHAPTER 28

*T*he vineyard seemed busier than usual, Avery thought as the car drove toward the house.

Marcus' car was parked out front. She grit her teeth. It was interesting how since day one, he'd had run of her home. Even before anything had happened between them.

She opened the door before the driver could even get out of the car. "You can put the bags inside the kitchen," she said, pointing, but continued walking.

Marcus was just inside the house in the small room she used as an office. "Welcome home."

"What are you doing here?"

"We have an appointment with your grandfather in an hour. Freshen up and meet me outside in fifteen minutes."

Avery looked around the small room. "Where are my personal things?"

"Pictures?"

"Yes, where are my pictures?"

Marcus sat back in the chair and let it recline slightly as he looked up at her. "This is your professional office where you will conduct business. There is no place for photos of old boyfriends."

She took a deep breath. "Why must I meet people here?"

"This is the vineyard. This is where everything starts."

Avery fisted her hands on her hips. "Marcus, where are my things?"

He stood and walked around the desk toward her. "They are stored. Now go upstairs and get ready to visit your grandfather." He reached for her arms and pulled her in to place a kiss on her lips. He didn't move until her mouth went pliant under his.

"That's better," he said as he pulled away. His dark eyes locked on hers. "Now we have less time. Please hurry."

Avery turned and headed for her bedroom. She'd been right. Everything had changed on that yacht. As she gathered her toiletries, she looked in the mirror and realized she didn't even know the woman looking back at her. It hadn't even been two months. Who had she become? Was this really the woman her mother was all those years ago?

Regardless of her mother's past this wasn't who she was now. Avery absolutely needed that trip home no matter what Marcus thought.

As THE SUN fell behind her grandfather's enormous house, she wondered how it was her mother had grown up there. Then she thought better of it. Her mother had been shipped off to boarding schools from a very young age. That was where she'd met Avery's uncle, Zach.

Avery smiled when she thought about it. A quiet American boy, her mother would always tell her. He was awkward and out of place. Her mother had fallen in love with him when she was just a small girl.

She contemplated that perhaps her mother and her uncle, who had married her father's sister Regan, were just like her and Pete. Though her uncle never felt about her mother the way she and Pete had finally admitted to feeling about each other.

But would that be how they would turn out? In-laws? Old friends?

Thinking about her mother having anything to do with the huge house in front of her, she began to miss the simple house her parents had raised her in. She thought of Ed and Darcy's house, which was her grandparents' old house. She thought of the house she'd moved out of that belonged to her aunt. How many Kellers and Bensons had lived there over the years?

The stories she'd heard were that the first romance from the basement was her aunt and uncle John.

The thought of Jill and Pete actually hooking up seeped into her consciousness and her chest ached. She'd told him herself that was how things worked—and then she moved away.

Who was this Jill? Who was this woman he was spending his mornings with? Was he spending his nights there too? A good friend, Pete had told her. She bit down on her lip and waited as the driver stopped the car, stepped out, and opened Marcus' door first.

Marcus stepped out of the car without another word to her or the driver. The driver came to her door and opened it "Thank you," she was sure to say especially in the absence of Marcus' words.

Marcus started for the front door without waiting for her, but when he looked back, she knew he'd wanted her to catch up.

"Make sure when your grandfather asks, you tell him about your investor meeting. Those gentlemen were hand picked by him to meet with you."

Avery nodded.

"He will want to know which restaurants were mentioned and which ones will have the first bottles of wine."

"I don't know that I remember them all."

"I will help you." Marcus stopped and turned toward her. "Your grandfather gave me his blessing with you."

She narrowed her eyes. "His blessing?"

"He thinks we are a fine fit together."

She puckered her lips as she thought. "I realize you think there is some grand affair going on between us..."

"Not an affair, Avery."

"Fine. Whatever it is, it's new. I'm a modern woman, Marcus. This hovering over me is making me a little crazy."

He stepped closer to her. "You came to be successful, yes?"

"Yes."

His lips turned up in a crooked grin. "I am successful. You will never need for anything but me and my last name," he said flatly then turned and entered the house without knocking or ringing the bell.

The entrance to the house was as grand on the inside as it was on the outside.

Her shoes clicked on the cold marble floor.

A man emerged from the library to her left. "Monsieur Pierpont will be down shortly. I have been asked to offer you a drink."

Marcus gave him a curt nod and followed him into the library. Avery followed, her hands clasped around her clutch. It had become a security blanket of sorts.

The man poured scotch over ice and handed it to Marcus. He then poured her a glass of wine without asking if it was what she'd wanted.

He then excused himself leaving Marcus and Avery alone in the oversized room.

"Do you suppose my grandfather will be long? I feel a headache coming on," she said setting her wine glass down on a small table.

"He will come when he is ready. You do not rush a man a busy as your grandfather."

And she wondered why he'd make them wait.

CHAPTER 29

*A*s it was, Marcus and Avery waited twenty-seven minutes for her grandfather before he walked through the door of the library. Avery's headache was nearly a migraine now clouding her focus and her sight.

"Marcus!" Her grandfather's voice echoed through the room. Marcus stood and moved toward her grandfather. "Always a pleasure to have you in my home," he said in French, but she'd understood it.

"Thank you, sir," Marcus smiled warmly as he shook her grandfather's hand.

Her grandfather then turned toward her, his eyes narrow on her, forcing her to rise to her feet. "Avery, I'm glad you could come." His voice had gone flat and it seared through her.

And that concluded the pleasantries.

The rest of the evening was pretentious hors d'oeuvres and precisely plated foods Avery couldn't identify. Her grandfather had an entire staff at his disposal and neither he nor Marcus ever thanked them as they served.

Conversation moved around her. The meetings she'd had with the investors were talked about in length, without her.

The onset of the migraine she'd had was now full blown. It absolutely exploded when she looked up and a fuzzy image of her grandfather was looking at her.

"You do agree, Avery?"

She couldn't help but just stare at the man. This man who had given her the very opportunity to be just like her mother, he was a stranger.

He wasn't as old as her Grandpa Alan. He wasn't as kind either. She missed her dad's parents as much as she missed everyone at home.

Suddenly the need to be with them was nearly as painful as the pounding in her head.

"I'm sorry. I didn't hear the question," she meekly replied.

His eyes narrowed again. This, she realized at this moment, was how he looked at her always. It was how he looked at her mother too.

"You and Marcus make a fine team. He is doing well over-seeing the vineyard and the winery. You are a good aide for him to have."

"Aide?"

He nodded slowly. "You are a pretty face. The image of my own daughter. She was good to have to interest business part-ners. I think the men enjoyed your company at lunch."

Her vision was nearly gone now, but she didn't know if that was the anger or the headache.

"I thought you bought the winery for me to run."

A smile formed on his lips. "Avery, you have your mother's fire. I assume you have her stubborn will as well," he said and the smile tightened. "A woman can entice business. Marcus can run it."

For a moment, she thought she might pass out at the table. She reached for her water glass and it shook in her hand.

"Avery," Marcus' tone was nearly sweet. "Are you okay sweetheart?"

"I have a headache," she said wincing. "A migraine."

Her grandfather leaned back in his chair with a grunt. "Her mother's mother would have those whenever we had a discussion that needed attention." He placed his napkin on the table and motioned for the man who stood patiently waiting by the door for some command. "Get her something for her headache."

The man nodded and disappeared.

"Maybe she should lay down," Marcus said, but he didn't move as though he were waiting for confirmation that it would be okay.

Her grandfather held up his hand. "They will get her something." He turned and that look seared into her again. "You are so much like your mother. You have not gone out and gotten pregnant have you?"

She wanted to be offended and she wanted to lash out, but the spinning of the room was making her sick.

"I need to get sick, Grandfather."

He let out another grunt as Marcus hurried around the table and rushed her down the hall.

The dinner and the wine came at her quickly and she released it all into the toilet as Marcus shut the door. Her skin broke into a cold sweat and she fell onto the cold marble floor.

At that moment, she knew what she needed. She needed her mother. She needed to go home.

"Avery, I have some pain medicine for you," Marcus said from the other side of the door.

"One moment."

She managed to push herself to her feet and rest her hands on the sides of the sink. Turning on the cold water, she took a small towel and wet it, then pressed it to the back of her neck.

When she felt the wave of sickness move on, she cleaned up and opened the door.

Marcus stood holding a glass of water and a few pills in his hand. "This should help."

She took the pills and the water then swallowed them down. "I want to go home."

He nodded. "The driver will take you."

She grit her teeth. "Fine."

Marcus moved in closer to her and touched her arm. "Is he correct, Avery? Are you pregnant? We didn't plan for you to be pregnant."

As painful as it was, she pushed her shoulders back. "No, I'm not pregnant. And if I was, it wouldn't be a crime either." She winced from the pain building behind her eyes. "I wasn't some mistake my mother just made. She loves my father and he's a very good man. He's an excellent father. My grandfather doesn't see that."

"Your grandfather has always been clear on what he thought was best for you and your mother."

Her blood ran hot in her veins. "I think I'm done here." She made a move to walk by him, but he stopped her, gripping her arms. The pain of it shot through her.

"He wants us to get married, Avery. Soon."

The air whooshed from her lungs. "Married? I haven't known you that long."

Marcus's eyes shifted. "Your mother had an affair with your father and got pregnant. He assumes you understand fast love."

"Are you saying you're in love with me?"

"Everyone can learn to love." His grip eased as he moved in closer to her nearly backing her up against the wall. "I know you still love that man back home, but that is over," he said sharply. "You know that and I know that, Avery. I can give you this life you have dreamed of since childhood. Cars, clothes, jewelry, exotic destinations. No one in Nashville can do that for you. You belong here. Inside of you, you are Pierpont. You are made for this. When we marry, then the winery becomes ours. It'll be our legacy to leave behind. Yours and mine." He traced a finger down her throat. "Marry me."

Certainly he wasn't proposing to her standing outside a bathroom where she'd just thrown up. This was about the most absurd thing she'd ever heard in her life.

"I need to go home, and I need to rest."

"You do not have an answer for me?"

"Marcus, this isn't what you want and you know it. It isn't what I want."

"But it is. I will give you the grandest wedding this area has ever seen, Avery. I promise you that. We will make a grand life together."

He moved in to kiss her and then shifted to kiss her clammy cheek.

"This is what will be, Avery," he growled the words in her ear. "You will be my wife and we will own the vineyard." He stepped back. "There is no need to answer me now. Your answer is yes, because you crave the power my last name will give you." His eyes narrowed when she gasped at his comment. "Go home. I'll be there soon. We will make arrangements."

If her vision was clear, she might have attempted to smack him. Had he simply decided they were getting married?

She walked away and toward the front door. Her arms still ached from where he'd gripped her tightly.

This man her grandfather wanted her to be with was a monster.

Avery was going to make plans, when she got home. But she was damn sure they weren't the ones Marcus wanted.

CHAPTER 30

*A*very's head still throbbed from her migraine, and the few lights in the car were making her dizzy. The pills would take affect soon, and she'd be okay.

Closing her eyes, she began to formulate a plan. She needed to get out of France. She needed to go back home. There was no feeling safe in France anymore.

Not knowing how long she'd have before Marcus came for her, she decided to stop at her house on the vineyard, quickly pack, and then drive toward Paris.

The throbbing in her head had subsided a bit, but now it spun with ideas. All of her credit cards were in her grandfather's name, and Marcus owned her phone.

She'd very quickly become a kept woman, she'd realized. One that could be wooed with luxurious vacations and plied with alcohol in order to do things she'd never have done.

No, that wasn't something she was going to dwell on. It was simply something she had to deal with—a battle of her conscious.

If she stayed in France, she'd just be some victim to Marcus and her grandfather. If she went home to Nashville, she'd never be alone.

The first moment she got, she'd call Spencer. He'd ask the fewest questions up front, but she'd be answering them all when she got back home.

Looking at the clock on her phone, she calculated the time difference in Nashville. Spencer would still be at work.

Avery waited until the driver had dropped her at home and driven away. The last thing she'd needed was him hearing her call Spencer.

The moment she walked through the door she dialed Spencer's number. A few transfers through the company and finally he answered.

"This is Spencer Benson."

"Spence," she tried to keep any terror out of her voice, but it had trickled through.

"Avery! I thought you'd forgotten about us. You haven't called me since before you left. Do you know the last time I went more than four days without talking to…"

"I need help," she interrupted.

"Avery, are you in trouble? Are you safe? I'll be there. Tell me what you need."

Tears burned her eyes, which only made the headache reveal itself again. This was her family. This was what she'd given up so foolishly.

"My credit cards are all in my grandfather's name and my phone is in Marcus'."

"Who is Marcus?"

That would be another thing she'd be filling him in on. "That's not important. I need you to wire me some money for airfare. I need to get home."

There was more going on with Spencer. Was he walking quickly? Was he running with his phone to his ear?

"Avery, what's going on? Tell me you're not in danger."

"I don't think I am."

"You don't think you are?"

"Listen, I'm a big enough girl to say I made a mistake coming here, and I need to get home. Spencer, I just need some money wired to me to get home. Now."

"Hold on," he said and then she could hear a muffled conversation taking place.

"Avery?" She cringed when she heard her uncle Zach's voice.

"Yes."

"I'm in contact with a colleague there who can fly you here. Can you get to the airport in Paris?" The tears that stung were no longer a threat. They flowed down her cheeks.

"Yes, sir."

"Are you with Monsieur Pierpont?"

"No. I left his house a half hour ago. I'm at the vineyard house."

"I'll arrange a ride if you need one."

"No, sir. I need to go now. I have a car."

"Are you in trouble? Is someone after you?"

She winced, thinking of Marcus grabbing her arms and making his demands. "No, sir. I just don't want to be here when Marcus arrives. I just want to go home."

There was a deep sigh on the other end of the phone. "Marcus Bravard?"

Her heart nearly stopped. "Yes. You know him?"

"His family." He let out another breath. "Are you and Marcus involved?"

What was she supposed to say? Her decisions, where Marcus were concerned, were as bad as her decision to move to France anyway.

When she didn't answer Zach simply said, "Well, let's get you home."

* * *

TAPPING his pen against his coffee mug, Pete looked at the clock in the boardroom. Seriously, could time go any slower?

Gail, the woman to his right, grabbed hold of his hand and stopped his tapping.

"You're going to make me crazy if you do that one more time," she whispered as his boss moved to the next frame of the presentation he was giving.

"Sorry," he whispered back.

Investments and the new trends in what's being bought were not on his mind. The beautiful girl in the basement with the soft curves, the infectious smile, and a booming laugh was on his mind. However, even that lovely thought kept getting interrupted by the words *I love you* floating through the phone that morning.

Avery had really messed him up.

How could she possibly still love him? She didn't love him enough to stay when he really needed her—and he'd needed her. No. She'd taken on the jet set life and vacations with Marcus.

She'd made good on her promise and called his mother. He'd gotten that phone call quickly enough with his mother ecstatically squealing on the other end of the phone.

It didn't stop the fact that it was time for him to forget about Avery and move on. How convenient was it to have Jill right there for him to do just that?

He was going to treat her right, he considered as he tapped his pen once more to his mug.

The heat from Gail's stare had him putting the pen on the table and placing his hands in his lap.

As his boss' voice dragged out the next best options for his clients, Pete thought about the night ahead. He didn't have to move on sexually. That wasn't what moving on was about. Oh, he'd take it if she offered, but he was thinking about impressing her first.

Music. Dancing. Flowers. Wouldn't she just flip if he filled her apartment with flowers before she got home?

He'd make some phone calls.

The room lit up as someone turned on the lights overhead. Pete realized everyone was getting up and gathering their things. He wasn't quite sure what the entire meeting was about, but he'd figure it out. He always did.

Gail handed him his pen as she gathered her items off the table. "Here, tap away."

"Sorry."

She gave him a smile and headed out of the room with the others.

Pete sat for a few more minutes planning out his evening with Jill. The thought, of moving on, had never seemed so appealing.

CHAPTER 31

*P*ete sat at the top of the steps, a bottle of wine in his hands, and two glasses. He'd seen Jill pull up and head down the outside steps to her apartment.

They'd unlocked the door between their places nearly two weeks ago, so he felt confident she'd be pleasantly surprised by his gifts.

"Oh, my goodness!"

She'd found them, and he was already grinning like a silly boy infatuated with a pretty girl.

He could hear her moving from room to room, gasping as she found another bouquet in each.

As he heard her move through the kitchen, he knew she was headed toward him. He put on his warm smile.

She gasped again as she turned the corner and found him on the steps holding the bottle of wine.

"Pete, what is all of this?"

"Me trying to impress you."

Her eyes were wide. "Okay, you did a good job."

"Glass of wine?"

The crease between her brows grew deeper. "Sure."

Pete poured each glass full then handed her one. "Here's to basement neighbors."

He sipped from his glass and watched as she processed the moment. Finally, she too sipped.

"I have dinner upstairs. Can I convince you to join me?"

She thought about it a few moments longer than he thought she should have, but eventually, she nodded in agreement and followed him back upstairs.

His mother had taught him a few dishes. He figured it was her way of helping him impress the right woman.

"What do I smell?"

Pete set his glass on the table, which he'd set properly, thanks to his mother again. "I have a lasagna in the oven." He pulled out a set of potholders, opened the oven, and pulled out the dish. "I hope you like lasagna."

"It's a favorite," she said smiling and then took a sip of her wine. "Why are you trying to impress me?"

"We've been hanging out for about a month and a half. Just feeling it out, I guess."

He pulled out a chair for her. "You kissed me this morning."

He couldn't help but smile as she sat down and then he sat next to her. "I did that."

"Why?"

"I don't think there is any secret that I'm attracted to you.

"You're attracted to me? Why?"

It was a silly question, he thought. Why wouldn't he be? She was wonderful.

"I think you're smart and funny. You make me laugh, and I've needed to laugh a lot this past month with everything going on in my life."

"I'm smart and funny," she said picking up her glass. "Haven't I heard that all my life?"

He'd pushed a button he hadn't meant to push. "I happen to

think you're extremely sexy too. I just didn't want you to think I was a pig, so I didn't start with that."

Now she smiled easily, as if he wasn't some freak.

"You think I'm sexy?"

"Very."

He cut a piece of lasagna and placed it on her plate, added a scoop of salad, and a piece of garlic toast. He then repeated the process on his own plate before looking at her.

She raised her wine glass to her lips. "I think you're sexy too, by the way."

"Okay, I think this is heading in the right direction."

Jill inched in. "And what direction is that exactly?"

"In the direction of non-bumbling neighbors trying to make passes at each other," he said scooping a bite onto his fork.

When she laughed, he found an ease to it. So far he hadn't scared her away. "You're not just trying to get me into bed, right?"

"No. Don't get me wrong. I'm a man. I think about it."

"You're also still in love with another woman."

He'd lifted his fork to his mouth, but stopped short of taking the bite. "What?"

Jill sat back in her chair, her wine glass in her hand. "You still love Avery."

It was matter of fact and out there. "Avery left me. She's hooked up with some guy named Marcus and they're having a wonderful life." He snapped his teeth against the metal of the fork as he took his bite.

"Are you sure it's wonderful?" She leaned in. "I saw your face when you talked to her this morning. Pete, she's still a part of you."

Now he took his wine and drank it down. "She always will be a part of me. She's been my best friend since I was seven. It just happened to be a mistake to finally fall in love with her."

Jill laughed. "Finally fall in love with her? Something tells me you've always been in love with her."

He set down his glass. "You're ruining my moving on," he whined.

"I don't mean to. Listen," she said rolling her glass between her fingers. "You've introduced me to her family. You've taken me to the bar with her cousins, dinner at their house, and you've talked about her for over a month. You're part of that family. How can you let her go?"

Pete reached for her hand. "Because I need to."

"And I'm your fall back?"

Pete stood as he kept her hand, then pulled her from her chair. "No. Never a fall back. I'm interested, Jill. You have no idea how much I want to move on, and I want to move on with you. And it's not about Avery. It's about how I feel for you."

She softened against him, wrapping her arms around his neck as he encircled her waist. "How do you feel about me?"

"Lucky that you haven't run away." He pressed his forehead to hers. "I want to feel this out. You've been on my mind a lot lately. That says it's important."

"I won't promise you anything. I'm not really good at relationships, okay?"

"Okay."

"I don't want it to go really fast either. A few more dinners. Maybe dinner with your family a few more times. You can come to my parents' house too. But I'm not falling into bed with you. And like I said when I met you, I could fall in love with you, but I won't."

"Will you kiss me at least?"

Her smile widened. "That I could do."

CHAPTER 32

*L*eaving the phone, watch, and the necklace Marcus had bought her on the bed, Avery drove to the airport in the car her grandfather had loaned her.

She'd have liked to have driven it somewhere else and taken a cab, but she was very sure they would quickly figure out where she had gone.

Just as her uncle had promised there was a plane waiting for her.

Paris' lights drifted away as a friend of her uncle's from childhood flew her toward Nashville—toward home.

Her headache had never quite subsided, so she took the opportunity to close her eyes and let the long flight become hours of rest.

She was quite surprised when she woke and discovered she had slept most of the flight. They were nearing Nashville in the wee early morning.

The thought that very soon she'd be wrapped in her mother's arms had tears streaming down her cheeks. How would she ever repay her uncle for his generosity?

A half hour later the plane landed and Avery shook with the

very thought that she was home. The air was different, and so was the sky from her view atop the steps that would descend to the tarmac. She wanted to kiss the ground when she made it to the bottom.

As she and the pilot stepped down onto the Tennessee ground, a familiar car drove toward them. The threat of tears was real now, and as her uncle's car came to a stop, her mother rushed from the passenger side and her father from the back seat.

She ran to them.

"Oh, Avery." Her mother held her tightly and her father embraced them both. "I have missed you. Tell me you are okay." She held her at arms' length and looked her over. "You are okay aren't you?"

It wasn't until that moment that Avery realized that when her mother was panicked her accent deepened.

"I'm fine."

"I told you not to go. I told you..."

Her father touched her mother's arm. "She's home."

Her mother nodded. "We need to take you home. You look so tired."

Avery nodded.

She saw her uncle speak to the man who had flown her home. They shook hands, shared a laugh, and she watched as Zach handed him an envelope.

How could she ever pay that debt off?

As her uncle drove them away from the airport, Avery rested her head against her mother's shoulder. No one spoke the entire drive home.

When her uncle pulled into the driveway, her mother unbuckled her seat belt. "I will make coffee. Yes, Zach, come in for coffee." She opened her door and hurried into the house.

Avery's father took her suitcase from the trunk. "I'll try to calm her down." He smiled at her as Avery climbed from the car. "You're okay, right? No one hurt you?"

"No, Daddy. No one hurt me. I was just wrong to think someone I never knew would embrace me."

He set her suitcase on the driveway and cupped her face in his hands. "You were embraced for who you are right here. Avery, what did we do that made you feel as though you needed something else?"

"I wanted what she had," she whispered.

Her father shook her head. "She didn't have anything until she had you." He kissed her on the cheek, picked up her suitcase, and walked back to the house.

Avery let out a sigh as her uncle came around the front of the car.

She lifted her eyes to him. "I don't think I can ever repay you for what you did for me."

Zach pulled her to him. "You never have to repay me. Your mother's peace of mind is payment enough."

Avery looked up at him. "She was worried."

Zach wrapped his arm around her shoulders. "She knew what you'd learn. Her father, though very powerful in the business world, is a horrible father."

That made her chuckle, but just as quickly she felt lost again. "I thought he'd let me become something important. But the vineyard was just another business to him. I never was given the opportunity to run or do anything."

"You were his face."

Avery turned to face her uncle. "His face?"

Zach nodded and leaned up against his car. "He used to send your mother to meetings. Investor meetings," he specifically added. "I suppose she was a distraction while he was gathering information. But she was never a vital part of his company."

"So he used me?"

Zach shrugged. "I don't know what his true plan was for you. But you mentioned a Bravard?"

"Yes, Marcus."

He nodded. "Long before your mother met your father, before I ever met Regan, your grandfather tried to set her up with a Bravard. They are a very wealthy family with a lot of connections. Your grandfather is all about connections, wealth, and power."

"Do you think that's why Marcus hovered over me as he did?"

"I would assume so."

"He asked me to marry him. Told me I'd be marrying him is more like it," she corrected.

Zach nodded. "That would solidify a union of assets in the end."

She felt raw inside. Her own grandfather had sold her out.

"I think I need some rest. I have a life to piece back together tomorrow—later today."

"We're all here for you, Avery."

"Uncle Zach, I owe you everything."

He laughed. "I think your mother is still paying off her debt from when I rescued her from your grandfather's house." He pulled her in one last time. "Having you two here with us is payment enough. Never give it a second thought."

He pressed a kiss to her forehead.

"I need to head home. Tell your mom I'll catch up with her later. Maybe over lunch."

"She does love to lunch."

"She always has."

He gave her cheek a loving pat and circled back to the driver's door, pulled it open, and climbed inside.

Avery had never been so thankful to have this family as she was tonight. Watching her uncle drive away she swore to herself she'd never doubt them again. Wanting to live with wealth and power was a silly dream. She had all the wealth she ever needed right there in Nashville.

CHAPTER 33

$\mathcal{A}$ song was stuck in Pete's head. He'd been dreaming about it all night.

As he forced his eyes open, he realized it wasn't just stuck in his head, it was actually playing on the TV.

The small moan from next to him had him smiling. Wrapped in his arms, pressed tightly next to him in her Wonder Woman T-shirt and shorts was Jill. Her hair fanned out over his shoulder and her breath warmed his bare chest.

They'd fallen asleep in the wee hours of the morning on his couch. Oh, they'd pay for that later when their muscles tensed. But for now he'd enjoy the warmth of her body pressed against his.

She'd been very specific that she wouldn't fall into bed with him. No one could honor that more than Pete. So they'd opted for movies in their pajamas, a whole lot of kissing, and at some point they'd both fallen asleep.

She stirred against him before lifting her head to look up at him. "Ah, we fell asleep," she slurred.

"Looks like it."

"It's Saturday, right? I'm not late for work," she mumbled against his chest.

"Nope. Lay here as long as you like."

She gave a low moan that had his body urging to do things she said she didn't want to do yet. So he took in a deep breath and held it.

"I should go to my place," she said on a laugh.

"You can stay right here all day."

"I have to pee."

That had them both chuckling.

"You could do that here. I swear my bathroom is clean."

Jill sat up, careful not to brush against him in the wrong areas.

"I'll be back in a bit. I'm going to go pee," she said smiling as she pushed back her mane of wild hair. "I'm going to brush my teeth." She covered her mouth with her hand. "And maybe my hair."

"I think you look beautiful just as you are."

"I'm finding you're incredibly complimentary." She pushed back her shoulders. "I'm going to hurt from sleeping in the crevice of the couch."

"I was thinking the same thing."

"Make me some coffee? I'll even bring my own stolen mug."

Pete grinned up at her as he laced his hands behind his head. "No need. I have more."

She gave him a nod and headed down to her apartment.

Perhaps he could move on, even though every time he kissed Jill, his heart ached just a little bit for Avery.

Pete stood and walked to the kitchen. As he pulled down the coffee filters and filled the pot with water, he realized he hadn't wanted to admit that to himself. Avery needed to be a memory of what had been, not what could happen. Jill was filling that void, and not just because she was convenient. Pete had a sincere interest in her.

He poured the water into the machine, placed the filter in the bucket, and filled it with coffee. It was going to need to be strong coffee. He was extremely tired.

That brought a smile to his face. He should be tired. It was nearly three in the morning before they'd fallen asleep with their lips swollen from kisses.

There was no need to rush anything, he thought as he pushed the button on the coffee maker. There was time to win her over.

He walked to the refrigerator and pulled open the door. Scrambled eggs were his specialty. Maybe he could win Jill over with some breakfast, wrapped up in a blanket on the couch.

The backdoor opened as he loaded up his hands with eggs. "I'm making breakfast. I hope you like scrambled eggs."

"Pete."

He froze bent over in the refrigerator.

Putting everything back on the shelf, he rose slowly taking in the moment.

When he turned, she was there. "Avery."

"Oh, Pete!" She ran to him and wrapped her arms around his neck.

It was instinct to pull her in and hold her, to smell her, to feel her.

"I've missed you. Oh, I've missed you so much."

He stroked a hand down her hair. "I've missed you too. Oh, how I've missed you," his voice was just a whisper.

Then he heard the unmistakable gasp from beyond them and his world spun into place as he looked up and saw Jill, still in her Wonder Woman T-shirt and shorts, her long, beautiful hair pulled back and a look of absolute horror on her face.

"Jill." He moved from Avery. "I thought—I was going to make breakfast. I…"

Avery's eyes had gone wide. "Oh. I'm so sorry." Tears welled in her eyes and she pursed her lips.

Jill formed a tight smile on her lips. "You must be Avery. I've heard a lot about you."

Avery stood there and Pete knew she was too choked up to talk. This was a moment he'd never envisioned.

"Jill, I didn't know that…"

She shook her head. "Don't. I should let you two be alone."

Jill turned to go back to her place, but Pete stopped her. His heart was exploding in his chest. How could he have such conflicted feelings right now?

"No. I should leave," Avery said as she bore a stare right into him. "I didn't realize…"

"Now stop." He held his hands on both sides of his head to keep the world from spinning. "Just stop."

How was he going to handle this? Two women who had two very different effects on his heart were standing there, and only one of them was suppose to be there. He wasn't sure which one, and he'd never been so conflicted.

Pete turned to Jill and took her hands in his, kissing her knuckles. "Can you give us a few minutes?" Gazing into her eyes he hoped he conveyed what he wanted to. A need to just talk to Avery.

Jill nodded. "Okay." As she turned, she looked toward Avery. "It was nice to meet you."

Avery's eyes were even wider and she bit down on her lower, pouty lip as Jill descended the steps. "I'm so sorry Pete. I didn't even…I didn't…"

"What are you doing here?"

"I'm back. I had to leave. It wasn't what I'd thought. I didn't know that…"

He moved to her as her wall crumbled around her and she began to sob. "Breathe."

She shook against him and sucked in a breath. "You're sleeping with your neighbor," she said softly into his chest.

"I'm trying to. We woke up together, that's all." He felt as though he needed to make that clear.

"She's lovely."

"She is. Where is your new man? I know you're involved Avery." The words were sharp and the sting in them bit him as much as he assumed it did to her when he felt her stiffen.

She looked up at him. Her dark eyes were bloodshot and sad. "I made the biggest mistake of my life leaving that day. And then I was just mad because you didn't come to see me off, and..."

"Is that what you think? You think I didn't come for you?" He pushed back and paced the kitchen. "You're so wrong, and so full of yourself to think that I'd just let you go."

"You didn't come, Pete. You let me go."

That was the final straw. "I came, damn it. I ran like hell to get to that damn plane. They wouldn't call you back to the gate and they wouldn't let me on. I wasn't going to let everything I'd wanted for my whole life just go away like that. Yes, I was mad. Yes, you broke my heart. But, Avery, I was there."

Her tears streamed down her cheeks, but he refused to pull her back in. She needed to know what heartache she had caused. "I needed you to be here for me and my family. My father went through surgery and you weren't there, but because of you he's alive. My mother is in chemo and she's scared to death. I'm trying to keep strong for her, but you're not here to keep me strong."

"The girl downstairs?"

"Yeah. She's here. She makes me laugh, Avery. She makes me happy."

She batted her eyes and wiped at her cheeks as tears fell.

"I'm so sorry, Pete. I needed to go. I needed to know what was there for me. I made a mistake." She looked down at the floor. "I made a lot of mistakes."

Her voice trembled and it hurt him. He had to move to her.

"What can I do?"

She shook her head. "Nothing. I've lost you."

The doorbell rang and Pete stomped his foot. "God, I hope that's not the mailman with a jury duty summons. That would make this day a total loss."

He huffed toward the door and pulled it open.

A man in a black suit stood just beyond the threshold.

"Mr. Grant?"

"Yeah."

"I am looking for Avery Keller. I am sure you know where I might find her."

The accent gave him away and Pete grit his teeth. "Oh, yeah. I know where she is."

Pete turned to look back at the kitchen and she was gone.

"Avery? Avery!" He moved to find her, but there was no sign of her. "Your guess is as good as mine," he said just as the man punched him right in the jaw and he fell to the floor.

"What in the hell?" Pete held his jaw.

"Find her."

Pete struggled to his feet. "Are you kidding me? I wouldn't turn her over to you if it was the last thing I did."

Marcus moved in closer to him and Pete put up his fists. "Fine, I know what you're made of now. Hit me when I'm ready."

Marcus stopped. "I want to speak to my fiancée. I know she came here and I'll wait for her all day if I have to."

Fiancée.

The very word made Pete nearly ill and the throbbing in his jaw worsen.

"I swear if you've ever touched her violently I'll kill you," Pete growled.

"A threat, Mr. Grant? No wonder she left you."

Pete would have made a move to strike the man, but just beyond Marcus, Pete could see a police car driving slowly down the street, pausing briefly in front of the house.

Marcus looked over his shoulder. "I will be back for her. Mark my words."

"She'll never be here."

Marcus gave Pete a curt nod and walked back out the front door. Pete quickly shut it and locked it as he watched the man give a nod to the police officer and then drive away in a rented black car.

"Avery!" Pete shouted. "Avery!"

Jill hurried through the kitchen, her face pale. "She's downstairs. She came running when she heard him."

"She's okay?"

Jill nodded. "She's scared, Pete. She had me call the police."

"They drove by."

She studied him. "Your cheek. What happened to you?"

"Don't worry about me. Where is she?"

"Hiding in my bedroom. I don't know what's going on, but she's scared of that man."

CHAPTER 34

*P*ete hurried down the steps to Jill's apartment.

"She's in the bedroom. I'm going to get her some water."

He nodded and then turned to her gathering her in his arms. "Thank you for helping her."

"Go. She's scared."

"Don't give up on me," he whispered.

"Pete, she needs you. I'll be in in a moment."

He kissed Jill softly and went to Avery.

She was curled up in a ball against the wall on the floor. Her hair hung over her face as if it were a shield.

"He's gone," Pete said as he sat down on the ground next to her.

Immediately she clung to him, wrapping her arms around his neck and pressing her face into his shoulder. All he could do was hold on to her.

"Here," Jill said as she walked toward them, handing Pete the glass of water. "I brought you some Advil too."

Avery looked up at her through ragged strands of hair. "Thank you. You don't have to be nice to me."

Pete chuckled as he brushed her hair back. "She doesn't know any different," he said smiling up at Jill.

"You guys take your time. I'm going to go up to your place and get that coffee. You have your privacy, but if you need me to call the police again..."

"I'm fine. Thank you," Avery said.

Jill nodded and quietly walked away.

Avery rested her head on his shoulder. "I see why you love her."

"I like her a lot. I didn't say I loved her."

"I love her. She could have sent me back up there. She could have told him I was here."

Pete moved so he could look at Avery. "I'll kill him if he hurt you."

She shook her head. "Just my pride." Her eyes moved so that she looked right at him and at that moment he knew she'd seen the mark Marcus had left on him. "He hit you."

"Superficial."

"Pete," she sobbed, clinging to him tighter. "It was all a business arrangement. My grandfather wants me to marry him. Marcus told me that there was no decision. We were just to be married."

"This isn't the turn of the century, Avery. He can't just do that."

AVERY THOUGHT about how kind and sweet Marcus had been to her when she'd met him. Then, how it all changed on the yacht when his words became more seductive.

She closed her eyes when she thought about him making the advances to her. The bottles of wine and champagne they'd consumed—she nearly choked on her breath. He'd forced her guard down and she'd become a victim to him because of her own pride.

"I never should have left. I should have stayed here and married you. I made a mistake."

His heart was so conflicted. No one, absolutely no one, would get away with hurting Avery. And at the very same time, she'd hurt him so much he wanted to leave her there crying in Jill's bedroom.

"Your parents know you're home?"

She nodded. "Uncle Zach arranged it for me."

And yet another blow to his ego, he thought. She'd called someone else to help her. Well, he'd give her that one. He hadn't been very cordial on the phone when they'd spoken and she'd ended the call with *I love you*.

Pete moved and rose to his feet, pulling her up with him. "Let's go upstairs and get some coffee. Let's clear our heads and formulate a plan. We need to keep you safe, and get that moron sent back to France."

PETE WALKED a step behind her up the stairs. Avery needed the comfort of his touch, but he was distant. There was no mistaking why. In the nearly two months she'd been gone, she'd nearly ruined her life and she'd lost the love of the only man she truly ever wanted.

Jill sat at the kitchen table with a mug of coffee, wrapped in a blanket to cover her pajama clad body.

Pete pulled a chair out for Avery. "Sit down. I can't doctor your coffee as much as you'd like, but…"

"Black is fine. I'll be fine without any fussing. Thank you."

He narrowed his eyes and went about pouring her coffee.

Avery finally looked up at Jill.

"Thank you."

"Me?" Jill rested her hand on her chest.

Avery nodded. "You didn't have to help me. I certainly didn't mean to walk in and ruin your morning. I know it was intimate and here I am."

Jill set her mug on the table and kept her hands wrapped around it. "You didn't ruin anything. Pete would have dropped everything had he thought you needed help."

She had to wrap her mind around that. From that statement alone, she knew that Jill knew a lot about her, and here she knew nothing about the woman who had moved into the basement.

Pete set a mug down in front of Avery then made a very grand point to walk around Jill, touching her shoulders as he did so, then sitting down next to her.

It was silly for Avery to get so worked up about it.

They'd been friends most of their lives, and the time they'd actually been lovers was very short in comparison. She'd been on double dates with him. She'd set him up on dates. How many times had they been double dating with boyfriends and girl-friends? There was no reason this should be so strange—except that she still loved him so deeply.

Oh, she knew she'd tried to move on, and she'd done it in the worst way ever. France was a mistake. Marcus was a mistake. Sitting there while Pete rested his hand on Jill's was a mistake.

She looked down into her mug. "I'd like you to follow me home. From there, I can have my dad and Uncle Zach work out something to keep Marcus from me. Uncle Zach still has connec-tions to my grandfather. My mother alone will..."

"Avery, we'll get you home safe. There isn't anyone in your family that's going to let you get hurt."

He winced when he said it, and she wasn't even sure he knew he touched his raw cheek.

"I've inconvenienced you both enough. I should get going." She pushed her mug back and stood.

Jill stood next, the blanket falling to the chair. "Don't run off. Avery, you need help and we're here to help you. I know he wouldn't let anyone hurt you, and the minute you leave, he's going to be pacing the floor worrying about you. Let him follow you home and talk to your family."

"You don't have to do this," Avery said. "You're involved and I'm the old girlfriend. I shouldn't have come."

"Are you kidding?" Jill moved toward her. "First of all, this is new for both of us and we're feeling it out. Second, I've spent nearly two months hearing him talk about you."

"Jill, that's not true," Pete argued.

She laughed. "Have you been here? Pete, everything in your life is about Avery. I just happened into the middle of it."

"You don't have to say that because she's standing here. She's the one who ran off and slept with some French guy."

Avery scoffed. "And you moved on right away too."

Jill shook her head. "Eh, not as quickly as you think. I'm not easy to get."

"And you think I am?" Avery argued.

Jill held up her hands. "Now the two of you need to have this argument. Not me. I'm saying, Pete, you need to follow her home and make sure she's safe. Avery, you need to get your shit together and press charges against this maniac who is chasing you down and beating up Pete."

Avery looked at Pete, who shook his head, and then to Jill who stood before her with her hands on her hips.

"I'm parked out back," Avery said softly.

Pete dropped his shoulders. "I have to get dressed." He turned and walked out of the kitchen and up the stairs.

Jill nodded. "I'm going to take my coffee and go back to my place." She started for the stairs. "Welcome home, Avery. Everyone has missed you and was worried about you."

As Jill disappeared down the stairs, Avery wondered how she would know how everyone felt. Who all had she met?

CHAPTER 35

*P*ete followed Avery to her parents' house and followed her inside when they collectively climbed from their cars.

Simone sat at the kitchen table with a legal pad in front of her and notes jotted down on it in French.

When she saw Pete follow Avery into the room, she rose and moved to him.

"She came home to us," she whispered in his ear. "She came home."

In the last month he'd hugged Simone Keller more than he'd held his own mother. Avery didn't need to know just how much they'd bonded over missing her.

Simone stepped back. "Avery, is everything all right? You look terrified."

Avery exchanged looks with Pete, and he gave her a nod.

"Mom, Marcus followed me here. He found me at Pete's."

"He didn't find you," Pete corrected. "He only came looking."

Simone studied Pete. "Did he hit you?"

"Cheap shot. He won't ever do it again, that's for sure."

He watched as tears formed in Simone's eyes. "Avery, you should have never gone."

"Too late, Mom. And I can't regret it more."

Simone turned back to the table and picked up the notepad. "A former associate to my father called looking for you."

"I'm not going back."

Simone nodded. "It seems as though my father purchased the vineyard and other property with investment money from the Bavard family."

"So."

"So, Marcus' need to marry you seems to be a business deal."

"I knew that. My own grandfather sold me out."

Simone nodded. "He tried to do that with me. Luckily, I fell in love and, well, I had you."

"So this is payback? Grandfather failed at the biggest merger ever because of me?" Her tone was sharp.

Simone shook her head. "Because of my choices. And, Avery, I'd always choose you first."

"So what does me marrying Marcus gain him?

Simone studied her notes. "Monsieur Bravard's ego is even bigger than my father's. Together they'd nearly monopolize many different industries. If you had provided them an heir…"

"It would be a solid deal and one person would inherit it all."

Simone shrugged her shoulders. "It cannot be that easy, but yes. Legally if they partnered they couldn't monopolize, legally. But an heir receiving it all, well…" She stopped and sucked in a breath. "Avery, I am so sorry that he did this to you."

Avery moved to her mother and held her tightly. "I made my own mistakes," she sighed. "Oh, did I make them."

Pete scrubbed his hands over his face, and then remembered the bruise that had formed where the asshole had hit him. "So you foiled his plans. Now what?"

Avery turned to him. "Now we have to make him go away."

"He flew all the way here to find you."

"I left without word."

"So you just need to tell him you're not going back?" Pete chuckled. "Why do I think he's not going to take that for an answer?" He touched his cheek. "Oh, that's why. The son of a bitch punches people who stand in his way."

"I don't have to marry him. No one can make me do that."

"Marriage or not, he's looking for the heir."

Pete watched as Avery's face lost color. Her mother took her hands in hers.

"There's no reason you'd be pregnant would there be?"

Pete looked away. "I should go." There was no way he could stand there and listen to Avery admit that there was some kind of chance that she might be pregnant with that monster's baby.

"Pete…"

"Don't." He held up a hand to stop her. "I'm glad you're home. I won't let anything happen to you. But you're safe here."

Without another word, Pete walked out of the house.

CHAPTER 36

*I*t wasn't even one o'clock in the afternoon and Pete had already had three beers. Before the day was over, he'd make sure he'd had enough to forget the day all together.

His stomach churned at the thought that not only had Avery slept with that maniac, but maybe she was pregnant. The thought made him absolutely sick.

"Are you drowning your sorrows?" Jill stood in the doorway, her hands on her hips.

"What is it when that woman is around, then my day goes to hell?"

"Another Avery conflict?"

He chuckled. "That's all it is with her. Conflict. Drama."

"And you didn't know this before you asked her to marry you?"

"It wasn't as bad before," he scoffed as he drank down the last of his beer and reached for another.

Jill moved in and stopped him from opening the next one. "Why don't we go for a walk? Get some take out? Anything. You don't need to drown your sorrows like this."

Pete narrowed his eyes on her. "Why did she drag me into this?"

Jill laughed. "Because she loves you. She trusts you. You love her."

"You keep saying that."

"It's true."

"And what about you and me?"

Jill smiled sweetly as she sat down next to him. She gently brushed her fingers over his bruise. "You and I are neighbors who have shared a whole lot of wonderful kisses."

"You're dumping me."

"I never had you. You've loved that woman since you were seven. How do you expect to just let that go away?"

"It needs to go away. It's a disease," he said as the backdoor opened and Avery walked through the kitchen and into the living room. "Just in case you forgot," he slurred. "You don't live here anymore. Why do you just walk in like—like you can?"

"Are you drunk?"

"Not as much as I want to be." He nodded his head toward Jill. "She took away my next one."

"Good," Avery scolded. "Here." She threw a small paper bag at him.

"A gift? For me?"

He let out a deep breath. The beer and anger had settled right into his stomach and he certainly wasn't feeling any better.

Pete opened the bag and pulled out a pregnancy test stick.

He noticed that Jill moved back from him and suddenly he couldn't breathe.

"Avery, what is this?"

"It's a pregnancy test, moron."

"I see that," he said slowly.

Jill moved back in slightly. "It's a negative test."

Pete looked at it, unable to read it, and then looked up at Avery for verification.

"She's right. It's negative. I'm not pregnant."

With Jill sitting that close, he didn't want to seem relieved. But he was.

"You're not having the goon's baby?"

Avery stood with her hands on her hips. "No. But see, they were worried I was pregnant. If I had been, it would have thrown off their plans."

Pete's head was swimming in cheap beer, but he was trying to piece together this conversation with the one they'd had at her mother's.

"So had you gone to France pregnant, it would have ruined all their plans to marry you off to the idiot who punches people."

She smiled. "Right."

"And that's what happened with your mother?"

Avery nodded. "My grandfather failed at setting her up with Marcus' uncle, it turns out. Instead, she ran off with my father and had me."

"Great. I'm very relieved you're not pregnant, by either of us."

Jill rested her hand on his thigh. "Pete..."

He backed off, but he could continue to argue with Avery. It felt better being mad at her than it did to be hurt.

Jill looked up at Avery. "Since I'm knee deep into this, let me see if I understand this. Your grandfather was trying to set you up with that man?"

Avery nodded. "It seems as though they are trying to marry the families together."

"Don't forget they want an heir so they want you knocked up by the *right* guy." His words slurred again.

Jill watched him and he tried to smile, but he simply didn't care that much.

She looked back at Avery. "You're your grandfather's only other heir? Aside from your mother?"

"Yes, and he disowned her when I was born."

"Lovely man."

Avery chuckled. "Right."

Jill threw her hands into the air. "You know what this means don't you?" She turned toward Pete.

"Her grandfather is a psychopath?" he said.

"Yes, but you need to knock her up."

The room went silent as both Avery and Pete held in breaths and stared at her as she laughed. "C'mon. You didn't see that coming? If Avery's married and having a baby, she can't marry that other guy."

"You didn't mention married," Pete reminded her.

"I didn't. But why don't you get married?"

There was no doubt his face mirrored Avery's. Her eyes were wide and her mouth had fallen open.

"You're telling us to get married?" Pete stared at Jill until she looked at him.

"Well, yeah. You were going to get married anyway. So get married now and when he comes looking for her she'll be taken."

The air simply expelled from his lungs. It was a stupid idea. Absolutely dumb—and yet perfect all at the same time.

Avery shook her head. "Jill, that's a sweet offer, but..."

"Offer?"

"Yes. I'm the one who walked away. I'm not going to take your boyfriend and marry him just to..."

"She dumped me three minutes before you came throwing pregnancy tests at me," Pete interrupted.

Avery's shoulders dropped. "Because of me?"

Jill stood. "What Pete and I had was fun. I was pretty sure it was never going to get too serious. Avery, he's in love with you. It's not like I'm giving him back. I never had him."

"Now, wait," Pete slurred as he struggled to stand. "You're dumping me and giving me back to her?"

Jill turned with her radiant smile. "Yeah. She needs you, Pete."

"Where was she when I needed her?"

Jill reached up and touched the cheek, which wasn't bruised. "She was finding herself. Women need to do that sometimes."

Pete looked at Avery, whose eyes said she was deep in thought. "Do you think this would work?"

"What?" Pete snapped.

"If we got married. We could annul it later, if you don't want to be married to me."

"That's an idea," Jill retorted.

Pete dropped his shoulders. "I think the two of you are freaking crazy. She left me. Now you're dumping me. I'm serious. This day sucks."

"It'll suck more if that man comes back for her, Pete. Protect her. You love her," Jill said as she kissed him gently on the lips, and walked back to her own apartment leaving him and Avery alone.

AVERY'S HANDS WERE SHAKING. She clenched them tightly as Pete simply stood there staring at her.

"I get it. I cost you Jill. I wasn't here for you. I left when I should have stayed. There is no reason for you to…"

"Why did you tell me you loved me on the phone?"

Avery's eyes widened. "You heard that?"

"Oh, I heard it."

Avery looked down at the floor. "I said it because it's true. I never had any intentions of getting involved with someone else."

"Intentions or not, you did."

Avery shrugged. "I did. I don't know how, but…"

"What do you mean you don't know how? It's not that hard to remember when you moved on."

"That's the problem. I don't really remember it at all," she said and her voice trailed off.

Pete's eyes grew wide as he moved to her and grabbed her arms. "Avery, you slept with the man."

She nodded, but it hurt to admit it.

"Did you consent to it?"

His eyes had softened and she could feel his gentle touch on her skin.

"I don't know. We were drinking wine with friends. We went back to his room and kissed. Then…"

"Oh, Avery," he pulled her to him. "I'm going to kill him."

"Pete, you can't say that. I was there. I let him kiss me—touch me. I…"

"You're going to marry me."

She pulled back and stared at him. "You don't want to do that."

"I do. I think it's the right thing to do. Like you said, if we need to we can annul it."

She nodded. "Right." She squeezed her eyes closed. "Pete, I do still love you and I don't expect after all of this for that to be enough. But, as your best friend, I can't tell you how much I appreciate this."

"It's not the first time I've been your escape clause to get you out of something you didn't want to do. Let's see where it goes."

CHAPTER 37

There had always been one great thing about Peter Grant being Avery's best friend—he was great with making plans.

The fact that it was already mid-day on Saturday, they'd need to wait to get a marriage license. However, if they caught the next flight to Vegas, they could obtain a marriage license the moment they got there.

It seemed cheap and cheesy, but Clara and Warner had eloped in Las Vegas.

She shook the thought from her head. This marriage wasn't real. It was convenient. Pete sat next to her on the plane with his arms crossed. It certainly wasn't going to be a romantic wedding.

Their plans were to return seven hours later to Nashville and then—well, who knew what would be next.

They hadn't told a soul where they were going, except Jill.

Of course, Avery had already decided she needed to buy a dress when they arrived. She couldn't just get married in her yoga pants. She didn't need anything fancy, just something that made Pete look at her as he once had. Once, before they'd fallen in love. She'd settle for that.

The moment the plane landed they stood to disembark. Without any luggage, they were able to just move from the plane and out to catch a cab.

Pete pulled his phone from his pocket and turned it back on. "You should check in with your parents."

"I'll have to use your phone."

"Where's yours?"

"Mine is in the ocean." She looked down. "The one Marcus bought me, I left there."

He nodded. "We'll get you a new one," he said with a near smile. "Here." He handed her his phone. "Just call them and let them know you and I are hanging out, but you're safe."

Avery nodded and made the call.

"You're with Pete?" Her father asked.

"Yes. We're spending some time together. But I'm okay. I'm safe."

"Where are you? I don't want that man coming after you."

Avery winced as she lied to her own father. "We're just going to hang out at Pete's and then go downtown. But I wanted you to know where I was."

"Okay," he said and she sighed. "I know you're safe."

As she said her goodbyes, Pete secured a cab. She turned off the phone and handed it back to him.

"You know, that's the worst lie I've heard you tell since our junior year," he said helping her into the cab and then following her.

"What lie was that?"

"When we all drove to Kentucky to camp at the lake."

The lake. She closed her eyes and remembered the weekend he was talking about.

"I hadn't thought about that in a long time."

Pete nodded, again crossing his arms as if it were his way of keeping them tied up and away from her.

"I think about it a lot. Technically it was the first time we *slept* together."

She laughed as she nudged him with her elbow. "Right, because I went up with...what was his name?"

"Troy," he said as if it were on the tip of his tongue.

"Right. I went up with Troy and he had other ideas about what that weekend was about."

"You didn't want to, so you slept in my tent."

"Has there ever been a day you weren't there for me?" The moment she said it she regretted it. "I'm sorry. I know you're the better friend."

"It's not a contest, Avery."

But she felt as though she owed him.

The driver took them straight to the county clerk's office.

The moment they walked through the door Avery gasped. "Do you suppose all these people are in a rush to get married tonight?"

"Looks like it," Pete chuckled. "Maybe they all have some mad man chasing them," he said as he took a number and waited for them to call them up.

With that, Avery sat silently next to him. It was an obvious reminder of why he was there with her at all.

"Is there anywhere specific you want to stop to look for a dress?" Pete asked as they finally left the clerk's office, marriage license in hand.

Avery shrugged. "I don't know this town very well."

Pete managed a cab, and as they drove away, he asked the driver to take them somewhere she could go shopping. Fifteen minutes later the driver dropped them off at the shops at Caesar's Palace.

"This place is wild," Avery said as she looked around.

"I'd take lower Broadway any day," Pete replied blandly.

Avery looked at the shops as they passed through the eclectic mall. "You don't have to shop with me. I'll try not to be long. I'm sure there is somewhere you can wait."

Pete stopped walking. "I don't want to let you out of my sight."

"Right." She hadn't thought about that.

As they passed by statues and the ceiling changed colors, she found a small shop with nice dresses hanging in the window.

"This looks nice. I think I'd like to go in and look."

Pete gave her a nod and followed.

She searched the racks for dresses that weren't too fancy, but would be useful in another situation someday.

"What about this one?"

She turned when Pete held up an elegant sundress. "It's simple, but you'll look radiant in it during the picnic season."

Her heart nearly stopped. He'd picked a dress, and not just one off the rack to get it over with. Pete had given it some thought.

Avery reached for it and held it in her hands. "I'll try it on."

Pete gave her a nod and walked toward a chair in the corner to wait.

The moment Avery slipped on the dress, she knew it was the one. It was gorgeous, and only made even better because Pete had picked it out for her. She'd take her small victories.

He was standing at the register when she emerged from the dressing room, the dress in hand.

"I found a shirt and a tie. You get me in my jeans and boots, but…"

"I think that's wonderful," she said, hoping her smile conveyed how special it was.

THEIR TIME WAS RUNNING SHORT. They had clothes and the license. Now they needed to find a chapel. "There's one just down the strip that has an opening," Pete said. "This is just a formality, so really it doesn't matter which one, right?"

"Right. We just need to get it over with," she clenched her teeth as she said it. When she'd thought about marrying Pete, it had never come with the bad feelings she was having now.

THE CHAPEL WAS TACKY, but as Pete had said, it was just a formality. Avery changed into the dress and tucked her travel clothes into her purse. She pulled a brush from her purse and gave her hair a quick fix, added some lipstick, and even a spritz from her travel atomizer she kept in her makeup bag. If this were a real wedding, she'd certainly have gone all out. But for spur of the moment, she thought she looked pretty good.

When she walked out into the lobby, Pete stood there waiting for her. His new shirt still had the fold marks in it, but the tie matched her dress and she thought he had to be the most handsome groom she'd ever seen.

"Avery, you look amazing."

She smiled. "Thank you. You do too."

"What, this old thing?" he joked and she felt the relief that they could have a normal moment. "Are you ready?"

She nodded and took his arm as they walked into the chapel together.

There were miscellaneous guests seated in the pews. Witnesses, she reminded herself. These would be the people who would sign off on this real wedding, which would lead to their sham of a marriage.

The man dressed as a minister, with large Elvis-like side-burns, began the short and sweet ceremony, but Avery didn't hear the words. Pete was standing next to her, his hands clasped in front of him. This was all just a promise to help a friend. It seemed cold and calculated.

"Do you Peter Grant take this woman to be your lawfully wedded wife?"

Pete looked over at her, and for the first time since she'd set eyes on him earlier that morning he smiled.

"I do."

Her heart rate picked up and even in this crazy moment she wanted to cry.

"Do you Avery Keller take this man to be your lawfully wedded husband?"

She took the breath and in her heart held on to the promise of the words. "I do."

"May I have the rings, please?"

Avery moved to correct him that they had no rings when Pete held a hand up to stop her.

From his pocket, Pete pulled her ring out and handed it to the man.

He appeared to bless it—perhaps appraise it—then handed it back to Pete.

Pete lifted Avery's hand and slid the ring on her finger where it had once adorned.

"Pete…"

"It was meant to be for you—my wife. This is no different."

Her tears wouldn't hold back now. They welled in her eyes and he stepped in to wipe them away.

The minister concluded his ceremony with, "You may kiss your bride," and Avery assumed Pete would kiss her cheek then step back.

Instead, he cupped her face and gazed into her eyes. "No matter the reason we're here," he said, "I love you, Avery Keller. I have since I was in the second grade. I'm proud to be your husband."

His lips pressed to hers in the sweetest, warmest, most intimate kiss she'd ever had.

CHAPTER 38

*A*very had fallen asleep on his shoulder as they flew back to Nashville. He'd caught her a dozen times looking down at her hand and admiring the ring on her finger.

If only it was all because they'd chosen to be together, Pete would be completely happy. But this was just to keep her safe. At what point would she need to find herself again? What would that cost his heart?

Once they arrived back in Nashville, they silently drove back to Pete's.

"What are your plans?" he asked as they walked through the back door of the house.

"I don't know. Would you consider letting me stay here? In the spare room that is."

He nodded. "You can have the main room. Really this is your place."

"Not anymore," she said as she heard footsteps on the stairs from the basement.

"Am I interrupting?" Jill poked her head around the corner.

Pete smiled when he saw her. "No. Come up. Want something to drink?"

"No, I'm heading out," she said quietly. "I wanted to let you know that guy came back by. He kinda just lurked around, he didn't knock."

Pete moved to her and took her hands in his. "He didn't talk to you did he? He didn't hurt you?"

"No. But I am going to go spend the rest of the weekend at my folks' house. Maybe a few more days until you know he's gone."

"Jill," Avery moved toward them. "I'm so sorry about this. I don't mean to cause you any problems."

"No problem. I don't want anyone to get hurt." She looked back at Pete. "You can take care of her, right?"

"Always have."

Jill nodded and backed away from Pete's grasp. She looked at Avery. "Nice dress."

"Thank you, it's my wedding…" She stopped and bit down on her lip. "I'm sorry. That was insensitive."

"My idea, right? I can't be mad."

Avery moved toward Jill and extended her hand.

Jill studied her for a moment and then shook it. "You are one of the most genuinely nice people I've ever met," Avery said. "I appreciate you, and I'm glad you've been here for Pete. He deserved to have someone like you around."

Jill smiled that genuine, infectious smile. "It was my pleasure."

Once again, Jill descended the stairs—only this time they heard the unmistakable sound of the lock on her door.

Pete turned to Avery. "I'm beat. I'm going to turn in. Do you need anything?"

She shook her head. "I'll be right up."

Pete started for the stairs. His body ached from exhaustion and his emotions were ragged from the many ups and downs the day had brought to him. If he could simply sleep for a week, he thought he'd like to try.

"Pete," her voice stopped him just short of the top of the stairs.

"I'm not sure I can ever repay you for what you've done for me today. I'm forever in debt to you."

He looked down at her, still in the dress he'd chosen for her. "Avery, you make sacrifices for the people you love, no matter how mad they make you and how long you hold on to the anger."

Sleep was difficult for Avery. The spare bedroom was in fact very uncomfortable. Of course, it could have been that her head was still buzzing with everything that had happened in the past four days.

All of the chaos, the expense, the anger, the broken hearts—it was all her fault. She sure had let everyone she knew down.

At some point in the deep darkness of the night, she'd finally drifted into dreams. Dreams of childhood, where Pete had hit her with the football. Dreams of teenage dances and long walks with Pete. She dreamed of their wedding, the one she'd planned, not the one she'd had. Each dream shifted into the other and peace calmed her mind and body.

Her dreams moved her back to the yacht and the sun on her skin. Pete brought her a drink and then pulled her in for a long kiss that made her knees weak. He turned her in his arms so they were looking out over the water at the railing. The waves began to build and the sky grew dark. She told him she was afraid. She wanted to go back home, and that was when Pete shoved her overboard into the water. The waves crashed up over her and all she could hear was the raging laughter from the deck of the boat —from Pete—as she sunk lower and lower into the darkness.

"Avery, wake up." His voice was clear, his hands on her shoulders.

Avery sprung up in the bed gasping for the air the water had stolen from her.

She heard him call for her again, "Avery, wake up."

His voice wasn't filled with laughter and it was close.

She took the breaths that she could and soon she woke.

Her breath came in gasps, but she could see him now, his face in the dark of the room.

Pete reached for her face and brushed back the wet strands of hair that clung to her skin.

"Breathe, baby. You had a horrible dream."

She stared at him.

"You tried to kill me," she croaked out the words, her voice raw.

"No. It was a dream," he said, his voice hushed and peaceful. "Nothing but a dream."

His hands were still in her hair. His body only inches from her.

"I was in the water." She took a breath. "You pushed me overboard."

"I would never hurt you. Not even in a dream." His hand cupped her cheek and he guided her to his bare chest where she rested her head.

"I don't want to be alone, Pete. I'm scared."

"I'm right here. I won't let you go. You're my responsibility."

She wanted to argue with him. She didn't want to be his responsibility that shouldn't even have been a choice of words. But she'd made it so when she left for France, when she'd turned him away, when she got herself involved with Marcus.

She'd take what he'd give her now.

"It's only three in the morning," he said. "Let's lie down and get some more sleep. I won't leave your side. Nothing will happen to you." He yawned as they lay back in her bed and she fell asleep wrapped in his arms, right where she always belonged.

The rhythm of his breathing, and his arms around her, allowed her to drift back to sleep. There were no more dreams of violent storms. Now there was only peace—just as there always was with Pete.

CHAPTER 39

*W*hen Avery opened her eyes again, the room was filled with daylight and she was alone in the guest room.

It was too good to have lasted all night, she thought.

Avery crawled out of bed wearing only a long T-shirt of Pete's. She found her yoga pants in her purse, slipped them on, and walked downstairs.

Chances were she couldn't convince him to run and get her a vanilla latte, but maybe he at least made coffee.

The house was quiet. There was no coffee brewed, no dishes in the sink. It wasn't until she heard voices outside that she realized Pete was in the front yard.

She looked out the window and saw him standing with a police officer. Cautiously, she opened the front door.

The officer looked up first, and then Pete turned his head.

"There's my wife."

The words were probably meant to be informative, but they washed over her—through her—and she felt as if she could walk on air.

He motioned to her to join them.

"What's going on?" she asked.

"Jill called the police yesterday when Marcus was hanging around. They're following up."

"Ma'am, we've been talking, and we think you should file a restraining order against the man."

"Oh, I don't…"

"Sweetheart," Pete said as he wrapped his arm around her waist. "I don't want anything to happen to you. I told him about the nightmare you had last night. You're scared."

"I made some bad decisions, that's all. I'm sure once he knows that I'm married…"

"Give it some thought," the officer interrupted. "We have the plate and description of the car. We'll continue to have someone drive by regularly."

Pete held his hand out toward the officer who shook it. "We appreciate it." They watched the officer leave and he turned her back toward the house. "They seem to think he's still around," he said opening the door. "I can't believe he's this persistent."

"I assume my leaving France has cost him more than his pride."

"Regardless, he's not touching my wife."

Avery stopped as they walked through the door. "I like when you say that. I can't help it. I don't expect you to stay married to me, not after what I did, but I like it."

He shrugged. "I guess we see how it goes. I have a lot on my plate. I've been going to mom and dad's to help around the house. Dad's doing good, but…well you know. And mom gets so tired and sick after her chemo. I've been working on some new accounts, and I hope they'll consider that promotion again."

She dropped her shoulders. "And here now you've run off and gotten married to help me out—again."

He moved back toward her. "I told you, when you…"

"Love someone. I know. But do you love me, Pete? Do you really, really love me?"

"At what point would you ever have doubted that?"

"I made myself doubt it. You didn't want what I wanted."

"No, I didn't."

She pushed a strand of hair from his eyes. "I didn't respect that," she said letting it sink in. "True love is respecting what the other wants." She looked up into his eyes. "Pete, what did you want?"

He moved to her and gathered her hands in his. "I'd wanted us to get married and be among our family as we started our own. I wanted that promotion I earned. I certainly didn't want all of this crap that has happened to my family, but I would have wanted you there with me while I was dealing with it. And..."

She pressed her finger to his lips. "I'm here now. I have your ring on my finger, and legally can use your last name," she said smiling. "I can't fix your relationship with Jill, but..."

"Avery, she was my distraction. I really, really liked her, but it was never the same. She knew that. I just refused to see it."

"Can we try to make this sham of a marriage work? Would you consider that?"

He brushed his fingers over her cheek. "Any marriage to you isn't a sham."

"I want coffee," she said off topic with a smile. "Did you make coffee?"

He laughed. "I did. At six o'clock. Honey, it's past ten."

Obviously the past week had caught up with her and wrapped in Pete's arms, again, she could let it go and rest.

"Oh, well, maybe we could go get breakfast, or brunch."

"Let's walk down the street and have bagels. Besides we have early dinner plans."

She narrowed her gaze at him. "We do?"

"Yep."

. . .

AVERY QUICKLY SHOWERED and dressed in another of Pete's shirts and her yoga pants. Even if she slept in the spare bedroom, if she were going to try and make things work with her husband, she'd need to move her clothes to the house. She couldn't keep wearing the same pair of pants.

She also needed to think about going back to work.

Though it wasn't her favorite thing to do, she'd worked for her mother's charity for years. Some contacts for their large gala every year still refused to talk to anyone but her. Certainly her mother wouldn't turn her down. Her father usually could find her work in the clinic he still worked in. Though that never appealed to her much.

One thing was for sure—she was never working in the wine industry.

When she was ready, she headed back downstairs. Again she heard voices, but these were familiar.

Pete stood in the kitchen with Jill. Though they stood side by side, they were distant. Jill had her arms crossed and Pete had his hands tucked into his pockets. They were laughing and Avery saw the spark in Pete.

It wasn't love. It was a deep friendship. He looked at Jill differently than he looked at her. Oh, he liked her, and she assumed that wouldn't go away. But she did make him laugh.

"Hey, it's your wife," Jill joked as she walked into the room. But she noticed Pete's smile as she had. It didn't fade. The moment, the smile, the look skipped in her heart.

"Hello, Jill."

"So how was the honeymoon?"

Avery would have thought the comment would have been snide, but it wasn't. Who was this woman who could capture Pete's heart and then comfortably give it back?

For a moment, she considered they were very much the same. Jill was a dear friend to Pete. Sure they hadn't known each other but a few months, but she'd become his confidant—his best friend when needed.

"Some honeymoon," Pete joked. "She slept in the spare room and then had a nightmare."

Jill's eyes warded concern. "Nightmare as in you were reliving something bad? Or were you just tired?"

"I think I've had a very taxing week and it all built up."

Jill nodded. "You might have a few more of them. It's a good thing you left France when you did. You didn't get completely into an abusive relationship that could have really ruined you." She tossed a look at both of them when they continued to stare. "Psychology minor. It fascinated me." She smiled sweetly. "Anyway, I think that idiot did enough mental damage to you. Luckily the physical wasn't a problem."

"Maybe not for her, but..." Pete rubbed his cheek.

Jill rested her hand on Pete's shoulder. "Something tells me that if he comes back around, and touches her, his face will look much worse." She pushed herself away from the counter she'd been leaning against. "Well, I have to go. Keep me updated on things."

She turned for the door when Avery stopped her and walked toward her. "Jill," she said holding out her arms and pulling Jill in for a hug. "Thank you for everything. You are another person I'll never be able to repay."

Jill chuckled. "Me? What did I do?"

Avery pulled back to look at her. "So many things, but you took care of Pete. You are his friend."

Jill shifted a look to him and he smiled. "Yep, I'll always be his friend."

She walked out the back door and down the outside steps, which also said a lot, Avery thought. She wasn't a free visitor anymore. She respected their privacy—their marriage.

"Okay, are you ready?" he asked, pushing away from the counter.

She stood for a moment simply looking at him. Life the past two months hadn't been what she'd expected. Even the good moments now dulled in comparison to the way Pete looked at her—had always looked at her.

Avery walked toward him and stood right in front of him looking up into those warm, dark eyes, which locked onto hers.

She lifted her arms around his neck and he responded by wrapping his around her waist.

"I can't make the past two months go away," she said softly. "But I want to try."

Pete nodded. "Let's get this maniac back to France, and then we can discuss what will happen."

She had to assume his answer would be something like that. He might love her, but it was going to take some time to earn back all his trust.

CHAPTER 40

*P*ete shifted a glance at Avery and admired the wedding dress he had picked for her. It was casual and probably the most lovely thing he'd ever seen her in. He had personally called her parents to tell them she was safe with him, and that the authorities had been notified of Marcus' stalking.

He'd taken her by his parents' house, though they agreed not to share the news of their marriage until they knew what was going to happen to it.

Pete's mother wept when she saw Avery walk through the door and his father pulled her in for the longest hug he'd ever seen him give anyone, and he thanked her for saving his life.

Pete was sure she was feeling appreciated now as they drove away.

"Your dad looks good," she said with her head rested against the back of the seat and her eyes closed.

"He does."

"Your mom has a beautiful head too. Not all people look good without hair, but she does."

Pete laughed. "Kacey and I told her that too, but she didn't believe us. You told her, and she actually beamed."

"We have a connection," she said.

That was when he took her hand and interlaced their fingers. "Yes you do."

Avery turned to look at him and smiled. She didn't say another word. That, Pete thought, was progress.

AVERY HADN'T ASKED where they were going for dinner. It was Sunday night, and when Pete turned down the street where her grandparents had lived, and now Darcy and Ed lived, she knew the plans.

"You've been going to Sunday dinner, haven't you?"

Pete smiled. "I told you once. I'm part of this family, and you're part of mine."

"I never should have forgotten that."

"In hindsight it only took you two months to figure it out," he chuckled as he pulled to the curb.

"Jill knew a lot about me. I assume you brought her to Sunday dinner too?"

Pete nodded. "She was very impressed that your family took her in as they did."

"They do that."

"I knew that. But she was in an awkward situation. Your parents are here already. I'm going to guess the whole house knows you're here, but they expect three of us for dinner."

"You should have brought her."

"She made it clear that we're just friends. Maybe someday she'll come again. Sadly, you've run out of cousins or I'd have set her up," he joked as he opened his car door.

Avery looked down at her hand. "Should I take this off?"

"Why would you do that?"

"I noticed your mother eyeballing it. She wasn't about to ask, though I'm sure you'll get a call tomorrow."

Pete grinned. "Avery, leave it on. They'll know why we're

married. Once Marcus leaves for France, and we know you're safe, then we can decide on what it means."

His words weren't meant to be cold, but she felt the snap in them. It was true, this wasn't the marriage either of them had planned. This one had a purpose and she hoped to hell it worked.

They both climbed from his car and walked toward the house. He hadn't held her hand again, but she understood. Things would remain awkward for a while.

Usually, someone was always looking out the window waiting for the next person to arrive. Today they walked all the way to the door and opened it without someone right there.

"Where is everyone?"

"Out back. House is getting a little tight to have everyone inside."

She chuckled as they walked through the house. As usual the kitchen was bustling with women. Her grandmother, now well into her nineties stood over the stove watching the sauces she made. Her aunt Madeline tossed a salad. Aunt Regan was cutting bread, and her mother, the least skilled in the kitchen, was sipping wine leaning up against the counter.

She'd seen them first, and moved right to Avery. "You're okay?"

Avery nodded. "I'm wonderful."

Regan saw her next and ran to her. "Oh, I'm glad you're here," she said enveloping her in a hug. "Zach told me about you leaving in the middle of the night. Oh, Avery. I'm sorry things went so badly. He was afraid for you the entire time."

Avery shifted a glance between her mother and her aunt. "History repeating itself, and I should have learned that my family was here. I don't know those others."

"You're home now," Regan said as she kissed her on the cheek.

Madeline and her grandmother kissed her, and she could hear the noises outside the backdoor. That was where her family was.

She took a breath. Was she ready to admit defeat to everyone?

"I forgot. I brought a few bottles of wine," Pete said. "They're in the trunk of my car. I'll get them."

Avery stopped him. "Let me go. I need a few moments to clear my head before I go out there."

Pete nodded and handed her the keys. "Take your time. No one is going anywhere."

CHAPTER 41

*A*very walked out of the house and down the front steps to the car. There was no reason for her to be nervous. She knew that. But for a moment they would all look at her different.

She opened the trunk of the car and pulled out the two bottles of wine Pete had tucked into a blanket to keep them from rolling.

She tucked one under her arm and the other she held in her hand as she closed the trunk.

As she turned around, she found herself being thrown up against the car, the two bottles of wine dropping to the ground.

Marcus' hand clenched around her jaw and his fingers dug into her skin.

"You betrayed me by coming back without telling me. No woman of mine betrays me and leaves my gifts just laying about."

"I'm not your woman. I am nothing to you."

He pushed himself up against her harder. "You are my ticket. There are no choices, Avery. You will marry me. I made it clear to you."

She tried all she could to shove him back, but he was much bigger, much stronger. "I would never marry someone like you. I never agreed to marry you. You can take your money and power and…"

"Get your hands off my wife." Pete's voice rang out from the porch of the house.

Marcus gripped her arms so tightly she was sure the blood had stopped flowing to them. "Your wife?"

Pete walked down the front steps followed by Spencer, Tyler, and Warner.

"I'll repeat it. Let go of my wife!"

Marcus leaned into her ear. "You think I am some kind of fool?"

"We got married yesterday. I'm untouchable to you now. I told you. I'd never marry you. I don't love you."

"This was not about love. You have betrayed me."

"One more time," Pete said as Ed and Christian filed out of the house. "Let go of my wife."

Marcus pushed her toward the car and she fell to the ground. He raised his fists as Pete moved in closer.

"Your army of weak men is nothing against me."

Pete moved in closer. "Not one of them will lay a hand on you," he said as Zach and Regan ran down the front steps followed by Simone and Curtis.

Marcus looked up as Simone moved in behind Pete. "You can tell my father that he has no power over my family."

Marcus shook his head. "You are dead to him anyway. You disgraced him."

"And I would choose that path again," Simone said.

"My uncle was too good for you, and I am too good for your daughter."

Avery saw the redness creep into her father's face.

Pete stepped in closer raising his fists. "You are a coward. You fight women. You punch when a man isn't suspecting. I'm here now. If you want to attack someone, you attack me now while I'm looking," he bit the words through gritted teeth.

"It would be my pleasure to bury you where you stand and make her watch what a weak man you are."

Marcus shifted to charge Pete, but Pete had been ready. He pulled back and with one swift blow he clocked Marcus right in the nose.

Blood spurted from him as he staggered back. Avery ran to Pete just as the police car sped down the street and came to a stop in front of the house.

The officers hurried in to take control of Marcus.

"Me? He is the one who hit me," he argued.

Jill's car pulled up behind the police car. She ran from it and straight to Avery. "Are you okay? He didn't hurt you?"

She looked down at her bare arms and bruises had begun to form where he'd gripped her. "I'm okay," Avery said.

"He came to the house. I was gathering a few things to take to my mom's. He broke in and I heard him. I didn't confront him, but I called the police. I was pretty sure he'd end up here once he drove away."

Avery pulled Jill to her. "You are a good friend."

Jill laughed. "I've been told that my whole life."

Pete laughed too. "Tell her she's sexy. She likes that one too."

Avery shifted a glance to Pete, who smiled down at her.

The police cuffed Marcus and threw him into the back of the car as he bled and cursed.

One of the officers walked toward Pete and Avery. "We have him on stalking charges, breaking and entering, and by the looks of your cheek and your arms," he said looking at Pete and Avery collectively. "I think we can certainly add assault charges to that."

Pete held his hand out to shake the officer's. "We appreciate this."

The officer nodded and looked at the crowd behind them. "Quite a group of witnesses you have here."

Pete looked behind him. "That's my family."

. . .

PETE STOOD in the yard until the police had driven away with Marcus. He looked down at his hand, which was still bloody.

"Here," Jill walked up to him with a wet rag. "Avery's mom is worried about you."

"I'm okay," he said taking the rag and wiping away Marcus's blood. "I'm glad he's gone. I can't believe men like that exist."

"They do. Too many of them. She's safe with you now."

Pete nodded then looked at his friend. "She is. I'll always keep her safe."

Jill smiled then swung her arms in front of her like a child. "So I got a job offer."

"Did you?"

"Did you know Avery's mom has a charity organization?"

Pete laughed. "You don't say."

"Yeah, they provide counseling to women who are trying to get out of abusive situations."

Pete nodded. "They do that, yes."

Jill gave him a playful shove. "Avery put in a good word for me to work with them."

"I think that would be wonderful."

"I knew letting you kiss me would lead to something good."

Pete pulled her into him and hugged her. "You knew all along we wouldn't be an item?"

She shrugged. "You loved her too much to let me in all the way. I love her too. I think you married the right girl."

"Stay for dinner?"

"Oh, you're too late," she smirked as she walked back to the house. "I was already invited."

Pete absorbed the moment before he walked in through the house and out back where his family gathered.

AVERY STOOD in the yard surrounded by all of her cousins, most of them holding a baby or two.

"I'm home. Just stop giving me a hard time," she laughed.

"It's what we do," Spencer argued. "You're a pain in our asses, and it is our duty to give you an exceptionally hard time about it."

"You most of all."

"I've had a damn pink and black birthday cake my whole life. I get to give you more crap than anyone."

Avery had missed this most of all. She loved each of these people more than she'd ever realized.

Pete walked up behind her and wrapped his arms around her waist. "You all giving my wife a hard time?"

Tyler chuckled. "We heard you tell him that. He believed you too, I think."

Avery looked up at Pete, who smiled down at her. "Actually, we flew to Vegas yesterday and got married. It was just to make it official so that Marcus couldn't argue the fact."

Simone pushed her way through the group. "You went off and got married?"

Clara snorted. "It's been done." She raised her hand and laughed.

Simone shook her head. "You didn't tell me."

"It's not like we were going to stay married. I told him we could annul it as soon as Marcus was out of the picture."

"I was giving that some thought though," Pete said as he turned her in his arms. "I mean, geez, we already got the license, did the ceremony, I gave you the ring. What if we keep the marriage?"

"Really?" She rested her hands on his chest.

"It would be a waste of time otherwise," he said smiling down at her.

"You still want me?"

"Nothing has ever changed, Avery." He kissed her softly. "But, for the sake of our families, I'd like to marry you again. A real wedding with a real dress."

Avery felt the first happy tear streak down her cheek. "I think I would like that."

Spencer stepped up to them pulling Julie by the hand. "Considering I have never, ever, ever done anything without you," he cleared his throat. "Julie and I were thinking about getting married next year on our birthday. Wouldn't it make sense if it were both of us getting married that day?"

"Double wedding?" Avery smiled through her tears.

"Pink and Black wedding cake?" Spencer offered.

Avery looked at Julie, who nodded and then at Pete. "What do you say?"

"Avery, I'd marry you in a cheap Vegas chapel on the spur of the moment," he kissed her gently. "Oh, I did that already." He smiled sweetly at her cupping her face in his hands. "This wedding sounds even better."

She pulled Pete in close. "Thank you for being my escape clause."

"Oh, honey, I've always got your back."

EPILOGUE

$\mathcal{A}$very secured the boutonniere on Spencer's jacket.

"I do think this is the biggest birthday party we've ever had," she said brushing her hands down his lapel.

"Did you see your cake?"

"Pink and black? Yes, I saw it. Did you see yours?" She joked.

"Avery, if you seriously got me a pink and black wedding cake..."

"For the first time, I thought of you and what you'd want," she said smiling at her cousin. "But we took a chance letting each other pick our cakes."

He laughed. "I took the biggest."

"Hey, birthday kids, are you ready?" Avery's father asked as he entered the room.

"I think I am, Daddy."

Spencer shook her father's hand. "I know I am. I'll go take my position."

Her father turned to her and gathered her hands in his. "You look beautiful, princess."

"I know this is a formality, and I've almost been married nine months, but I'm nervous."

"So is your groom," he said grinning.

"I can't believe it took me so long to realize he was the one."

Her father kissed her on the cheek. "You're lucky he waited."

"Okay, here's your other bride," Courtney said as she and Julie walked through the door.

"You both look radiant," Avery said.

Courtney did a little spin. "Do I? I'm very afraid my breasts are going to leak if I hear Fitz cry."

Avery laughed at her cousin Tyler's wife. "If you need to feed him during…"

"Um, no. That isn't going to happen," Courtney laughed as Clara walked in and touched Courtney's arm. "Okay. My seeing eye Clara is here. I'll be up there when you two get there."

Avery looked at Julie. "Thank you for sharing your day with me—with us."

"You and Spencer are like brother and sister. I can't even imagine the bond you have. I think this is the perfect way to celebrate that."

Avery's father stepped up to both of them and kissed each of them on the cheek. "Are you ready?"

"I most certainly am," Julie said with a radiant glow to her smile.

"Yes," Avery said on a deep cleansing breath. "I'm ready."

Avery's father offered them each an arm and walked them to the door of the chapel.

Clara and Warner stood to the side of the pulpit, each with a guitar. Upon her father's nod, they began to play.

It wasn't a traditional wedding march, but that had been the plan. Their gift to each couple was to write a song that celebrated the love between Julie and Spencer and Avery and Pete.

The little church was filled with family. Avery thought it was a perfect way to celebrate Julie as well—since she had no family of her own.

Pete's nephew carried rings and his niece scattered flowers on the ground as their mother urged them to the front where they would all stand.

Avery thought the sight before her was grand. Pete and Spencer watched as they walked toward them. Was Pete crying? Spencer was.

Standing with them was Pete's brother Craig and of course Tyler, Eduardo, and Christian. On the other side, a row of weeping new mothers, dabbed their eyes. Courtney, Darcy, and Victoria were stunning in their bridesmaids' dresses. Pete's sisters Kacey, Sarah, Jenny, and Dawn each wore a rose in their hair to symbolize their family bond.

When they reached the altar Avery's father kissed each bride and handed her off to the man who would forever love and take care of them.

"You look stunning," Pete whispered in her ear. "Even more so than the day we got married."

The minister began the ceremony and Avery absorbed every moment that the blissful day had to offer. A year ago she'd been planning her escape. She had no idea she'd escape back home to where she belonged—with her family.

Clara and Warner sang each couple a song as they lit unity candles and recited their vows to each other. Then Spencer exchanged rings with Julie and then Pete's nephew offered his pillow of rings to the minister.

"Peter, repeat after me."

The minister said the words which Pete repeated as he gazed into Avery's eyes. Then he took the ring and slid it on Avery's finger.

She looked down to admire the ring she'd loved for nearly a year, but it wasn't the same.

She lifted it to take a closer look.

When she gazed back at Pete, he was smiling wide. "You deserved a little something new."

"It's gorgeous," she said looking back at the new ring. The

diamond was twice the size and embedded in a ring of birth-stones, which represented both her and Pete.

"I promise to change out one of those birthstones for each child we have," he whispered.

"No escape now, is there?"

"None. I've chased you since I was seven. I'm never going to let you go and I'm never going to make you want to leave."

They continued with the service once Spencer gave Avery an elbow to her arm to get her to continue.

The minister closed his book and looked at each couple. "I now pronounce you each man and wife. Gentlemen you may kiss your brides."

Spencer scooped Julie into his arms and dipped her for a long and breathtaking kiss.

Avery laughed as she looked back at Pete, who cupped her face with his hands and gazed deep into her eyes.

"Thanks for inviting me to stay for your birthday last year."

"Thanks for staying."

"Always," he said before mimicking Spencer's kiss on his new bride.

As both couples turned the minister announced, "Please welcome Mr. and Mrs. Spencer Keller and Mr. and Mrs. Peter Grant."

As the church broke into glorious applause, Avery looked around.

Her grandparents sat in the front pew holding hands, their foreheads pressed together. It had all started with them. The two people who showed generations what it was like to love forever and accept everyone as family.

Avery had never been so proud to be a Keller. Now she could instill those same values into her own family—the one she would have with her very best friend. This was a marriage that would never need an escape clause.

We hope you enjoyed Bernadette Marie's *The Escape Clause* as well as the entire *Keller Family Series*. Continue the family saga with an excerpt from the bonus novella, *A Romance for Christmas*.

INTERNATIONAL BESTSELLING AUTHOR

BERNADETTE MARIE

A ROMANCE
FOR CHRISTMAS

A KELLER SERIES NOVELLA
BOOK ELEVEN

BESTSELLING AUTHOR OF
THE THREE MRS. MONROES TRILOGY

A ROMANCE FOR CHRISTMAS

A KELLER FAMILY SERIES NOVELLA

he neighborhood looked just as it had in the conceptual drawings that hung on the wall in the construction trailer nearly two years earlier. Tiffany would always be grateful for the job Spencer Benson had given her. Sometimes it paid, and paid well, to have successful friends.

She had sold most of the houses in the development. It had netted her a nice condo and a hefty shoe collection. Driving back through the neighborhood always felt as if she were coming home.

Tiffany admired the holiday decorations that were unique to each home. Twinkling lights of multi-colors, or bright white strands of lights illuminated the entire street. The trees that lined the neighborhood were decorated too. Christmas was in full swing.

She couldn't help but wonder if each family she'd sold a house to, during development, still lived in each of the houses. The babies that were due after closing were now walking, she thought. The toddlers would be starting Kindergarten. New families had moved in, and original ones had moved out. That was how a neighborhood was supposed to be.

But she wasn't there to visit one of the cookie cutter builds her dearest friend Spencer had designed and built. She was driving through this neighborhood to get to his custom-built home, which sat just behind the Hart Estates, which he'd named after his great-grandfather.

She passed the well thought out park near the entrance of the community and drove past the paths, which in the summer were green and lush to walk on. The barn behind Spencer's house came into view, and a moment later so did the grand house Spencer had built for his wife, Julie.

Tiffany sat at the stop sign for a moment and took in the sight of it. The barn was laced with white twinkling lights, which matched the house with its wrap around porch. It was magically mesmerizing.

From a block away she could see the enormous twelve-foot tree in the arched window. Tiffany liked glamour, and this house had it all. To think she'd once thought she'd be in line for that— the house that Spencer built. That had been long ago, a distant thought, by a young girl who dreamed of being Spencer's wife.

She let out a breath and turned her car toward the house.

Who was she kidding to say she thought she'd have been Mrs. Spencer Benson? They'd been friends far too long. They had loved equally as long. No, she'd lost him the moment he saw Julie walk into the boardroom during a business merger. From that moment on, Tiffany was only the best friend and that was all she'd ever truly wished to be.

She loved Spencer's wife Julie—loved her like a sister. They had grown extremely close the past two years. Julie and Spencer belonged together. There was no question about it.

Tiffany pulled her car up behind a long line of others, and turned off the engine. She was her casual late—which she preferred. She liked to make an entrance.

Pulling down the visor, she opened the mirror. Her red hair shimmered with a touch of glitter she'd added. It was festive, she thought as she pressed her lips together to freshen the shine on them.

Picking up the pearl pink bag in the seat next to her, she looked it over. *Tiffany's Treasures* was scrolled in gold foil on the bag.

Things weren't so bad, she grinned. She may not have gotten the wealthy and sexy man she'd vied for so many years, but she was living her own dream. Once people had seen the wedding ring she'd designed for Spencer to give to Julie, orders for Tiffany's custom jewelry began to pour in. It wasn't but a few months before she was able to open her own jewelry boutique.

Inside the bag were special Christmas gifts she had designed for the Bensons. Each gift was as unique as the friends she was giving them to.

Tiffany opened the door and stepped her high-heeled foot into the thin layer of snow that had fallen. Someone was bound to comment about her footwear, but she couldn't help herself. She was addicted to shoes.

Besides, this was a party and she was there to enjoy herself. There was a room with her name on it on the second story of the house. If she celebrated too much, she'd stay.

Slowly, and carefully, she walked across the street and up the steps to the house.

Tiffany pushed open the front door of the house Spencer had designed. Laughter and conversation filled her ears. Spencer's cousin Clara was the first to see her.

With a toddler on her hip, and a growing pregnant belly, she hurried toward Tiffany and enveloped her in her arms, the toddler pressed between them.

"Merry Christmas," Clara said over the noise in the house.

Tiffany felt the warmth of the holiday in the sentiment. "Merry Christmas."

"You look beautiful," Clara said as she looked at her. "You're always stunning."

"So are you," Tiffany said, resting her hand on Clara's stomach. "I didn't know about this one."

"This is what living on your husband's tour bus will get you," she giggled like a girl telling a secret.

"How is Warner?" she asked of Clara's famous musician husband.

"He's so busy. He's been on tour for six months straight. Luckily he's in Nashville for two weeks until after Christmas. He's playing the Opry tomorrow."

"That's fabulous."

"Then it's back out on the road for a few more months, but I'll be staying here until the baby is born."

Tiffany couldn't even imagine Clara not having her husband around, but then again Clara was part of the Keller/Benson clan. No one was ever alone.

Clara took Tiffany's hand and pulled her further into the house. "I have tickets for tomorrow. You should come. An Opry show is always the best."

"I'd love that."

"Warner has a new bass player too. I'm not going to tell you how sexy he is. That would be wrong for a married woman with a baby and a pregnant belly to say such things. But he's here, so you can mention to me later what you think."

Tiffany laughed as she walked toward the living room.

Just as she had imagined, all of Spencer's cousins and their spouses, and their kids, filled the room. Spencer's brother Tyler stood with his wife Courtney and their two children in the corner. The children were watching the lights twinkle on the Christmas tree and she could hear Tyler explain the site to his wife, who was blind.

"Tiffany, you look beautiful."

She turned to see Spencer's mother Regan walking toward her. She pulled her to her and squeezed her tightly. "I stopped into your store the other day," she said. "You weren't there, but the designs you've created are amazing. I bought a pair of earrings that I just had to have. A Christmas present just for me." She pushed back her hair to show off the pearl drop earring.

"You deserve that. And thank you for the compliment. I love what I do."

"It shows."

"You're all crowding her," Spencer's voice rang over the others. "Let me at her."

Years ago he'd have gathered her in his arms, lifted her in the air, and planted a loud kiss on her lips. But that was old news. Now he hugged her, with one arm, and kissed her on the cheek.

"Merry Christmas, Red." He called her a name he hadn't used since childhood, referring to her hair color.

"Merry Christmas."

"Thanks for being here."

"I'd never miss it."

Julie pushed her husband out of the way and wrapped her arms around Tiffany. "You're here!"

"I wouldn't have missed it."

"Come here, I have something for you," she spoke over the noise and pulled Tiffany by the hand through the kitchen and out the back door.

"Where are we going?" Tiffany laughed as she balanced on her shoes, which were not made for running.

"Just out the back." Julie pulled her out to the porch and shut the door behind them. She huffed out a breath that carried on the cold air.

Tiffany looked around. "What am I looking at?"

"Me! I'm pregnant."

Tiffany felt her body fill with the warmth of pure joy for her friends. "That's wonderful. I'm so happy for you" She hugged Julie. "Why are we out here?"

"Spencer wanted you to know first, but I wanted to be the one to tell you. We're going to tell the family tonight."

If the tears that threatened actually fell, Tiffany was sure they would freeze.

"I'm so happy for you both. I really am."

"I knew you would be. Okay, now I'm freezing," Julie laughed as she pulled Tiffany back inside the house the house where Spencer stood with a glass of wine.

"For you," he said handing it to her.

Tiffany leaned in and kissed him on the cheek. "Congratulations."

"Thanks," he said smiling. "Okay, now that you know we have to announce it. You were first."

She rested her hand on her chest. "You don't know what that means to me."

Spencer took Julie by the hand and they walked toward the living room. Tiffany kept back and sipped her wine in the kitchen.

"Have you ever seen this many people in one house?" A man she didn't know walked into the kitchen. He was tall and his muscular build threatened the integrity of the fabric of his T-shirt. His hair was long and pulled back in a ponytail low at the base of his neck. At least four tattoos were clearly visible on his arms and he wore a leather bracelet on his left wrist.

"They have a very tight knit family. I've been around them all my life," she said, drawing her attention back to the crowd in the other room.

He nodded as he drank from his red plastic cup. "I got dragged here, but they're all nice enough."

"Who drug you here?"

"Warner. I'm playing bass for him and my family is in Canada. He said I needed a dose of family."

"You'll get it here."

So this was the bass player. She'd certainly have to confirm to Clara that the bass player was in fact very sexy. It would always amaze her that the members of Warner's band had a bad boy look to them. This one was no different. Strong and sexy with a little mystery behind those eyes, and a ponytail she wanted to give a tug.

The thought humored her.

"I'm Tiffany," she said holding her hand out to shake his.

"Blake."

"Nice to meet you, Blake," she said as they both leaned against the counter and watched as the family gathered around Julie and Spencer for their announcement.

"What are they doing?"

She figured it wouldn't hurt anything to tell him. "They're announcing their pregnancy."

"Oh, that's deep." He glanced at her. "How do you know that?"

"I'm Spencer's best friend."

"You? Men and women can't be best friends."

"Sure they can. I'm proof. I'm very close to Julie too."

He let out a hum. "No disrespect, but I couldn't just be your friend," he said, sending a look over her. "I'd always be thinking about you in other ways."

Sexy, but typical, she thought. "Spencer and I used to be involved. But he loves Julie. I want him to be happy."

"Are you happy?"

She looked at Blake, who had amazing blue eyes. But no significant words surfaced as she stared at him. "I'm happy," she finally said.

"Are you sure?"

Who was he to ask her such questions? "Of course I'm happy. I have a great life. I'm doing what I love and I'm making a living at it."

The corner of his mouth turned up into a sexy grin. "Me too."

Okay, so they had that in common.

She knew the moment the announcement had been made. Spencer's mother burst into joyful tears and his cousins flocked the couple.

Tiffany took a long sip from her wine and let it soothe her.

There was nothing she wanted more than Spencer and Julie's happiness. But this idiot next to her made her wonder if she was truly happy.

She was. Everything she'd ever wanted in life, she had. Her business was wildly successful. The second bedroom of her condo was a full walk-in closet with no less than two hundred pairs of designer shoes. The car out front was a Mercedes and paid for.

But as she watched Spencer's brother Tyler lean in and kiss his wife, each of them with a baby on their hip, she felt the sinking feeling that eventually won over. She didn't have a family of her own.

PLEASE REVIEW

We hope you enjoyed *The Escape Clause* by Bernadette Marie. If you did, we would ask that you please rate and review this title. Every review helps our authors.

Rate and Review: The Escape Clause

ABOUT THE AUTHOR

Bestselling Author Bernadette Marie is known for building families readers want to be part of. Her series The Keller Family has graced bestseller charts since its release in 2011. Since then she has authored and published over fifty books. The married mother of five sons promises romances with a Happily Ever After always...and says she can write it because she lives it.

Obsessed with the art of writing and the business of publishing, chronic entrepreneur Bernadette Marie established her own publishing house, 5 Prince Publishing, in 2011 to bring her own work to market as well as offer an opportunity for fresh voices in fiction to find a home as well.

When not immersed in the writing/publishing world, Bernadette Marie can be found spending time with her family, traveling (mostly to Disney parks), and running multiple businesses. An avid martial artist, Bernadette Marie is a second degree black belt in Tang Soo Do, and loves Tai Chi. She is a retired hockey mom, a lover of a good stout craft beer, and might have an unhealthy addiction to chocolate.